"It wouldn't matter to me how 'tasty' Pedro is," smiled Amy. "We're just being nice to him for Michael's sake." She waved a finger at Hannah, as a joke warning. "So just you remember that, Hannah."

"*Moi?*" giggled Hannah. "*I'm* not interested in him. Why should I be?" She cuddled up to Callum. "Not when I've got my hunky redhead. It's *you* I'm worried about, Amy. After all, it's *you* who's going to be alone for five weeks."

"*Hola!*" yelled Pedro as he hurried down the path towards them, dressed in red shorts and white T-shirt.

Amy stared, open-mouthed at the gorgeous face, the dark brown eyes below the short, jet-black hair, the dazzling white smile . . . and the strong tanned legs.

"Hi!" she gulped. "So you're Pedro!"

~~A~~ Love NOTEBOOK

Love dreams

Denise Colby

■ SCHOLASTIC

For Denis Bond

Scholastic Children's Books
An imprint of Scholastic Ltd
Euston House, 24 Eversholt Street
London, NW1 1DB, UK
Registered office: Westfield Road, Southam, Warwickshire, CV47 0RA
SCHOLASTIC and associated logos are trademarks and or
registered trademarks of Scholastic Inc.

First published as *Love Letters* by Scholastic Publications Ltd, 1997
This edition published in the UK by Scholastic Ltd, 2009

Text copyright © Denise Colby, 1997

ISBN 978 1407 11158 2

British Library Cataloguing-in-Publication Data
A CIP catalogue record for this book is available
from the British Library

The right of Denise Colby to be identified as the author of this work
has been asserted by her.

Printed in the UK by CPI Bookmarque, Croydon, CR0 4TD
Papers used by Scholastic Children's Books are made from wood grown
in sustainable forests.

3 5 7 9 10 8 6 4 2

www.scholastic.co.uk/zone

One

Amy gazed from the third-floor Art Room window towards the courts where the year-twelve boys were on the last round of their tennis tournament. Taking out a tissue from the pocket of her white shirt, she pushed back her blonde fringe and gently dabbed the sweat from her forehead. It was the hottest July she'd known; uncomfortably hot . . . and yet, when most of the pupils at Melthorn High were looking forward to the end of term and their trips to the coast and open-air pools, Amy had no such longings.

She had a place at college but, unable to find a temporary job, she'd decided to stay at school, helping Hannah to design the set for next term's pantomime.

Hannah approached and stood beside her, smiling knowingly. "I bet I know who you're watching," she said. "That's the *real* reason you stayed on at school."

Amy smiled too, her eyes never leaving the hunky figure leaping around the tennis court, his blond hair flapping across his stunningly bright blue eyes. She sighed. "Yes. Pity he doesn't know I exist," she replied.

Hannah put her arm round her best friend's shoulder. "Of course he does, Amy," she said, softly. "Michael's just shy, that's all. I mean, have you ever seen him talking to *any* of the girls?"

This was precisely why Amy had taken a shine to him. He wasn't pushy, like so many of the other boys in year twelve. Throughout the year, many of them had approached both her and Hannah to ask them out. But then that seemed to be almost customary at Melthorn High. The year-twelve boys would date the year-eleven girls. And even though these boys were only one year older, they always appeared to be so confident.

"Why don't *you* ask *him* for a date?" suggested Hannah, with a broad grin. "After all, you haven't got long. Three weeks. Then you may never see him again."

"I know. I know," sighed Amy. "Don't remind me."

Miss Butler, the art teacher, entered the class and saw the two girls staring through the window. She came over to them and followed their gaze across the tennis court. All three watched as the stocky blond boy, dressed in white shorts and T-shirt, thundered across the court and whacked the ball straight into the net.

"There's a lot to do, girls," Miss Butler said softly. "Time to take your eyes off the boys, eh?"

In the distance, Michael turned and looked up at the sky, noting the clouds just beginning to eclipse the sun. Amy and Hannah leaped back from the window with a squeal. They wondered if they'd been seen, staring down at him. They followed the squeal with a burst of giggles.

Miss Butler gave them a mock scowl. "Come on, girls," she said. "Let's get on with these designs. You can continue boy-watching at lunchtime."

Callum held back his head and opened his mouth, filling it with the warm water running from the communal shower until his cheeks swelled to bursting. Michael glanced sideways at his best friend who was, as usual, acting the fool.

"Aren't you ever going to grow up, Callum?" grinned Michael as he ran the soap over his tanned chest.

Callum squirted the water into the air and laughed as it sprayed over the shower ceiling and down on to his head. "I'll grow up when I leave here," he said. "When I have to get up at six in the morning and go off to work."

Michael turned to face the tall, slim boy, handing him the bar of soap. "I thought you were going to university?" he said. "So, what's changed?"

Callum took the soap and rubbed it into his spiky red hair.

"Well, it depends, doesn't it? If I don't get the grades then I can't, can I? I'll end up working in my dad's garage instead."

Michael grimaced at the thought. He hated anything to do with cars and he could never understand how Callum could get so excited about fiddling with engines and getting covered with oil.

"I'm not Mr Brainbox, like you," Callum went on. "I'll probably fail the lot."

Michael turned off the shower and reached for his towel. "Of course you won't. I bet you end up with better grades than me." He began to roughly dry his blond hair. "Then you'll be off to university . . . and still be acting like a ten-year-old."

Callum also grabbed for a towel and began drying himself. "Still, one thing's for sure," he said. "I'm a better tennis player than you."

Michael laughed loudly. "Give over! I won the match."

"Aah, but only because the sun was in my eyes," Callum grinned. "It was glinting off the Art Room window."

Michael playfully flicked him with his towel. "Bad loser," he said. He left the shower and crossed into the changing-room where his clothes hung on a peg.

Callum followed him. "I bet you didn't see *her*, either, did you?"

"Who?" asked Michael. He sat on the bench under his peg and began to dry his feet.

"Amy."

"Amy?" Michael's heart began to race.

"She was watching me . . . thrashing *you* out on the court."

"Give over."

"Honest," said Callum. "She was staring out of the Art Room window. Her and her friend. That Hannah with the long black hair."

"But who says she was watching *me*?" asked Michael.

Callum shrugged and grinned. "Yeah. Perhaps it's me she's after. Let's face it, I'm sure she'd prefer a tall lanky ginger-nut to someone like you." For a few seconds his eyes saddened. He knew there was no way he could ever compete in the romance-stakes with someone as good-looking as Michael.

"I really like her, Callum," Michael said, seriously. "I think she's lovely." He reached for his shirt and began to get dressed. "I wish I could talk to her," he added.

Callum lectured his best friend: "Be bold. Just go up to her and ask her out. You can take her to the cinema . . . or McDonald's, or . . . well, *anywhere*. But if you don't ask her soon, then you've had it! She's leaving school in three weeks."

The lunch bell went.

"Great," said Callum. "I'm starving. Are you having a school lunch today?"

"Yes," Michael replied softly. He wondered if Amy would

be in the canteen. And he wondered if he could summon up the courage to sit at her table.

"Don't look now!" Hannah mumbled through a mouthful of pizza, as she peered through her black fringe. "He's just come in with Callum; that tall, ginger-haired boy."

Amy flicked a sideways glance across the canteen towards the main door and saw Michael heading for the food counter.

"Perhaps he'll come and sit here," added Hannah. "And then you've *got* to say something to him."

Two year-nine boys approached and plonked their trays down on the girls' table.

"We're saving those seats," Hannah said sharply. "Go away."

One of the boys sneered. "You can't save seats. It's not allowed." He took his place opposite Amy and began to eat his dinner. Then he looked across and gave her a cheeky grin. "Want one?" he asked, offering her a soggy chip, dangling from the end of his fork. "I've put vinegar on it."

Amy giggled. "No thanks," she replied, kindly.

Hannah stared at the boy who was about to offer *her* a chip. "No!" she said aggressively before he had time to speak. "Can't you go and sit with kids your own age?"

The boy put the chip in his mouth and smirked at her.

"Too late," sighed Callum as he and Michael turned from the counter carrying their trays. "I thought that was our chance. We could've sat with them. Then you'd *have* to say something to her."

Michael smiled, resignedly. "Another day," he said.

He and Callum sat at an empty table on the other side of the dining-hall and began to eat.

"Give her a look," said Callum. "She'll never know you're interested unless you make it obvious."

Michael attempted a quick glance across the hall, but as he did so, Amy reached out for the salt and missed his faltering advances.

Hannah nearly choked on her pizza. "He looked at you," she said. "He looked straight over here. He *does* know you exist. I *told* you."

Urged on by Callum, Michael looked across again, this time catching Amy's eye.

Amy returned the look with a coy smile . . . and Michael quickly looked away. The fork in his hand was trembling as he scooped up a mouthful of potato.

Callum was amazed. "You're shaking," he gasped.

Michael felt embarrassed. His face went red. "My arm's just shaky from playing tennis," he lied.

Callum's eyes twinkled. "You sure?" he said.

Michael rapidly began to down his food. "Come on," he said. "Let's get some sun on our bodies. It's stupid sitting around in here."

"Do you want me to go over and tell her?" asked Callum.

"Tell her what?"

"That you fancy her and that you want to take her out."

Michael was horrified. "No way!" he said. "I hate all that 'my friend fancies you' stuff. It's humiliating."

"Shall I go over and say something?" asked Hannah.

"Like what?" asked Amy.

"Like you think he's the most gorgeous bloke in the school."

"You dare!" Amy warned her. "If I decide to chat him up, I'll do it without your help, thank you, Hannah."

The year-nine boy grinned at her through a mouthful of tomato-ketchup-soaked burger. "You can chat *me* up if you like," he said, sounding half-serious. Then he added, "Go on. Have a chip."

Michael took off his shirt and lay on his back. Most of the upper-school students who used these old amphitheatre steps beyond the tennis courts for sunbathing during the summer term, were silently reading.

"You should take yours off too, Callum," Michael said. "Get some sun on that pale skin of yours."

"I can't," replied Callum, irritably. "You know I burn." He enviously eyed Michael's golden chest and stomach. "You don't realize how lucky you are," he sighed. "I wish I could tan like that. I just turn pink."

"It's a good job you're not coming to Spain with me then, isn't it?" said Michael. "I can't wait to get there."

Callum shrugged. "I'd be better off holidaying in Iceland," he said. "With a bag over my head."

Michael laughed.

"You'll be all burned up to a little crisp if you lie out like this in Spain," Callum warned him. "It's dangerous, you know. People going on holiday abroad are always being warned."

Michael turned on his side and leaned up on one elbow, facing Callum. "How many more times?" he said. "I'm not going on holiday. I'm going to study. I won't even *see* a beach where I'm staying."

"It's a pity she won't see you when you get back, looking like Adonis, isn't it?" smiled Callum.

"Amy?"

"Yes. She'll probably be doing some dead-end nine-to-five job somewhere," he continued. "She'll be earning money and going out with some guy she works with by then." He laughed. "Like a real grown-up! Not like you and me . . . the eternal students of Melthorn High."

"She might be going to college," said Michael. He sat up. "Are you sure she's not coming back to do her A levels?"

"She's definitely leaving," Callum assured him. "I've been asking around."

Michael eyed him suspiciously. "You sound as though you're pretty interested in her yourself."

"I was asking for *you*," Callum grinned. "I thought you'd want to know." He stopped suddenly, tightly gripping Michael's arm. "She's over by the tennis courts," he said. "She's coming this way."

Michael immediately lay on his back again.

"What are you doing?" hissed Callum.

"Playing it cool," Michael replied.

"Playing it cool?" Callum gasped in disbelief. "Freezing her out, more like. Don't be stupid. You'll never get to talk to her at this rate." He could see the pulse beating in Michael's bare chest. "You're scared stiff!" he added.

Michael quickly sat up again. "No, I'm not!" he said, defiantly.

To Callum's surprise, he got to his feet and, holding his rolled shirt in his hand, he began to head towards Amy and Hannah.

Hannah croaked, "He's walking towards us!"

Amy turned and began to walk back towards the upper-school entrance.

Hannah followed close on her heels. "I don't believe you!" she snapped. "He obviously wants to talk. Why are you running away?"

Amy quickened her pace. "I can't, Hannah," she said,

looking back over her shoulder. "I don't know what to say to him."

Michael stopped in his tracks and stared after the two girls. He turned and dispiritedly strolled back to where Callum sat, open-mouthed.

"What happened there?" asked Callum.

Michael sat. "I don't know. She saw me and just turned back."

"Perhaps she's as nervous as you are," suggested Callum.

"Oh yeah?" replied Michael. "It's obvious, Callum. She just doesn't fancy me."

He lay on his back, closed his eyes and felt the warm rays of the sun burning into his reddening cheeks.

Halfway through the afternoon, Callum found Michael in the library, engrossed in a Spanish verb book. He sat beside him and whispered, so as not to disturb the students around them. "I've got an idea."

Michael closed his book. "Tell me."

"A letter," said Callum. "You can write her a letter."

Michael sighed. "A love letter? Oh *please!*"

"What's wrong with that?" asked Callum. "You know how good you are at English. Write her a letter, asking her out . . . and we can leave it in her form-room desk."

Michael shook his head, unsure. "I don't know."

"Go on," Callum urged him. "Look, I'll help you to write it." He began to sound excited. "We can keep it simple. You haven't got to make it all lovey-dovey or anything like that. Just say that you like her and ask her if she's free to go out one evening."

"I'm not sure," Michael said softly.

"Of course you are," Callum argued. He opened his bag and took out his large writing pad and a pen. "Come on, Michael. It could be your last chance."

He placed the writing paper and the pen on the table in front of his friend.

"But I don't even know how to start," protested Michael.

Callum put the pen into Michael's hand. "How about, 'Dear Amy. . .'?" he said.

TWO

Hannah and Amy decided to walk to school rather than take the bus. Even at eight-fifteen in the morning, it promised to be yet another boiling day. As they approached the gates, Amy checked to see if Michael was around. He was often on early morning prefect duty, stopping the lower-school pupils from taking the short cut across the teachers' car-park.

"We're too early," grumbled Hannah. "He won't be here until half-past."

Amy smiled. "We should've walked slower."

They headed for their form room, intent on grabbing the books they needed for the day, before returning to the school gates and making their entrance for a second time.

"We've got to make it look as though we've just got off the bus, though," suggested Hannah as she scooped up her maths folder and her chemistry textbook from inside her desk.

"Mind you, even if we came face to face with him, you'd probably go all shy again and run away."

Amy was silent, gazing into her desk at the neatly-folded square of white paper with her name on it.

"What's up?" asked Hannah.

Amy opened the letter and stared wide-eyed at the signature on the bottom of the page, before reading its contents.

"What is it?" asked Hannah, impatiently.

Amy silently handed her the note.

Hannah read what Michael had written and squealed with delight. "I don't believe it!" she gasped. "He wants a date."

"What do I do?" asked Amy, nervously.

Hannah sighed. "What do you mean, 'What do I do'? You say 'yes' of course. You arrange to meet him somewhere." She grabbed her general notebook and sat at her desk. "Come on," she said, "let's write him a reply."

"You can't come this way!" yelled Michael at the girl who was approaching from the gym block and crossing towards the out-of-bounds car-park.

Callum grabbed the sleeve of Michael's white shirt. "It's Hannah," he said. "That friend of Amy's."

Michael gulped. "D'you think she's found the note already?"

Callum grinned. "Looks like it."

Hannah, acting ultra-cool, came right up to them. "I know I shouldn't be coming this way," she said, staring into Michael's bright blue eyes. "But I'm only being a messenger."

She handed him a folded note, smiled at him, winked at the open-mouthed Callum . . . turned and nonchalantly walked on towards the school's year-eleven entrance.

"What's it say?" Callum asked excitedly.

Michael opened the note. "I bet she's not interested," he said, softly.

He read what Amy had written:

Meet me outside the tech block after school.

"Well?" asked Callum.

Michael smiled. "So far, so good."

Amy stood at the side of the technology block, trembling. She'd laughed loudly when, earlier, Hannah had asked if she should accompany her. Now she wished that she'd said yes.

Michael left Callum in the cloakroom and crossed the playground towards the tech block; his heart pounding and his mouth becoming drier and drier by the minute. Callum had told him exactly what to say . . . and now he was rehearsing the lines over and over again as he slowly approached the beautiful blonde girl in the distance.

As he reached her, he smiled . . . and said nothing, worried that the carefully planned words would just come out as one long croak.

She smiled back and spoke. "Hi!"

"Hi!" he said. "You turned up then?" It was a stupid thing to say, and he knew it.

"It looks like it, doesn't it?" she replied, sounding just as awkward as him.

He put out his hand. "I'm Michael." What *was* he saying?

She laughed and took his hand, shaking it formally. "I know," she said. "You're Michael and I'm Amy." She knew that she'd have to take control immediately. His palm was running with sweat and she noticed the nerve in his cheek which gave an involuntary twitch. He was obviously even more nervous than her.

"I have to catch the eighty-one bus," she said. "Do you want to walk me to the bus stop?"

She immediately began to worry that Hannah might still be there, waiting at the stop.

"Good idea," he said. "I have to go that way home, anyway."

They walked across the school playground towards the main gate, keeping an arm's length distance between them, desperately trying to find things to say, both hoping that they weren't boring each other with mundane tales about school life and their transport home . . . and the amazing warm weather.

From the top of the road, Amy saw the familiar figure of Hannah, leaning against the bus stop, her bag at her feet. Michael saw her too.

"There's your friend," he said. "Are you travelling home with her?"

Amy knew that if she stopped at the bus stop and began talking to Hannah, that would be *it*! He'd say his goodbyes, walk on . . . and the opportunity would be lost for ever. She grabbed at her only chance.

"Actually, I don't live very far away," she blurted out. "I'm down on the Belling Estate. I could walk it from here."

His heart began to race even faster. "I could walk you right home if you like," he suggested. "It's on my way," he lied, hoping that she wasn't aware that he lived in the opposite direction.

"That would be nice," she said. "We don't have to pass the bus stop," she added quickly. "We can cut through the Grove."

Hannah lifted her head when she heard the bus approach. At the top of the road, she saw Michael and Amy cross at the roundabout and walk on past the post office into the Grove.

By the time they'd reached Amy's front door, the subject matter of their conversation had moved on to their likes and dislikes, their favourite bands . . . and what both of them did in their spare time.

"You could come in for a tea or coffee or something if you want," Amy said, surprising herself at her boldness.

"Great," said Michael.

He followed her down the hall and into the large kitchen at the back of the house.

"No one home?" he asked. He wished he hadn't said that. He wasn't meaning to imply that he was glad that they were alone together. "It's not that. . ."

She smiled at him as she began to reach for the kettle. "Mum'll be home from work soon," she said. "No. There's no one in."

She filled the kettle under the kitchen tap.

"So you're leaving school at the end of term," he said.

"Yes," she replied. "How do you know?"

He shrugged. "Oh . . . people talk. A friend of mine told me. My friend, Callum."

"The tall boy with the ginger hair?" She got two mugs from the rack and put some coffee in each of them.

"Yes. He's my best mate. He told me. . ." He hesitated. "He told me that if I didn't ask you out soon, then it'd be too late." There! He'd said it!

She faltered as she screwed back the lid on the coffee jar. Her fingertips felt numb; her mouth was dry.

"That would be nice," she stammered. "Where shall we go?"

She blushed.

He blushed too. "I don't know. I. . ."

They heard the key turn in the front door. "It's only me!" called a voice.

"My mum," Amy said to Michael.

"Should I go?" he asked.

She panicked. She didn't want him to leave. "Why?" she asked.

Amy's mother came into the kitchen and was surprised to see the good-looking boy being entertained by her daughter.

"This is Michael, Mum," said Amy.

Mum nodded. "Hello, Michael."

"He's in year twelve, doing his A levels," she said quickly.

Mum took off her coat. "Wise boy. Can't you persuade my daughter to stay on and do *hers*?" she smiled.

Amy tutted. "I'm going to college," she informed Michael. "I want to be a children's nurse. It's what I've always wanted to do."

"At least she's got a nice, long summer break before she starts, haven't you, Amy?" Mum said.

Amy glared at her, warning, "Mum!"

Mum sighed. "All right. All right." She turned to Michael. "Her father wanted us all to go away for the summer. The south of France. We used to go camping there every year until Amy suddenly decided that camping was a little unsophisticated for her."

Amy laughed. "It wasn't that at all, Michael," she explained. "I just thought, what with starting college in September, I'd be better off spending my time here, seeing friends and stuff."

"*I'm* going away," Michael said suddenly.

Amy's heart skipped a beat. "Really?" she said, trying not to sound too concerned. "Where?"

"Spain," he said. "I'm doing Spanish as one of my A levels, so I'm spending the summer there."

"The whole summer?" asked Amy, dreading his reply.

"Yes. I'm off in three weeks and I don't get back till September."

"That'll be fun," said Amy, forcing a smile.

Mum saw the far-away look in her daughter's eyes. "Kettle's boiling, Amy," she said.

"Are you sure you don't want to stay for something to eat?" asked Amy as she saw Michael to the front door.

"No. I'd better be off," he replied. "Mum'll be cooking something for me."

She felt desperate, as he began to walk down the path towards the road. He hadn't repeated the offer of taking her out. She wondered if he'd changed his mind.

He turned at the gate and came back. "So, are we going out then?" he asked.

She beamed. 'When?'

"Do you like Decoy?'

'They're not my favourite group," she laughed. "But yes . . . they're all right."

"They're playing at the Granville tomorrow night," he said. "Have you ever been?"

She'd been once, when Hannah had insisted they'd go . . . and she hadn't liked it at all. It was dark and smoky and loud. Certainly not her sort of club.

"Yes, I have," she replied.

"Do you like it?"

"Yes. It's great," she said.

"Tomorrow night, then?"

"Great."

"I'll pick you up about eight. All right?"

"OK." She laughed. "I'll see you tomorrow at school, anyway."

"No you won't," he replied. "I'm not going in tomorrow. I haven't got any lessons. And I can do my private study better at home."

She was disappointed. School would be very dull, knowing that he wasn't somewhere in the building.

"See you, then," he said.

"See you.

He kissed her quickly on the cheek; a shy, furtive peck. And as he strolled off along the path, she closed the door and waited a few seconds, composing herself before returning to the kitchen to be greeted by knowing looks and a broad grin from her mother.

As soon as he'd turned the corner, Michael ran like the wind; through the Belling Estate, past the Oval Shopping Centre and across the park to Callum's house. He stood panting at Callum's front door, having hammered loudly three times on the brass knocker.

Callum opened the door and gasped. "You're sweating like a pig," he said. "And you're as red as a beetroot."

"Can I come in?" Michael asked urgently. "I've got a problem. I mean . . . *we've* got a problem."

Both boys climbed the stairs to Callum's bedroom, littered as usual with CDs and textbooks and writing paper.

"So, how did you get on?" asked Callum. He sat on his bed and began to chew on a half-eaten chocolate bar which he'd thrown down when he'd heard Michael's frantic knocking.

Michael sat beside him. "She's fantastic," he said. He laughed. "I'm so in love!"

Callum grinned. "Oh sure. Love, is it? Already?"

"No, honest, Cal, she's really nice."

"Apart from being stunningly beautiful, of course."

"Of course," said Michael.

"So, did you actually *speak*?" asked Callum.

"Yes. We talked a lot," Michael informed him. "I know everything about her."

Callum looked at his watch. "In an hour and a half, eh? And you know everything?"

"And I've asked her out," Michael said, confidently.

"Good on yer!" laughed Callum. "Well done, mate!" He slapped Michael's knee. "I was beginning to think you didn't have it in you."

"Well, I've proved you wrong, haven't I?" Michael said, proudly.

"So when are you going out together?"

Michael fell silent.

"Michael?"

"That's the problem, Callum."

"Not tomorrow night?"

"Yes, 'fraid so."

"But we've arranged to go to the Granville to see Decoy," sighed Callum. "You and me. I've got the tickets, Michael."

"I know. And that's the other problem I've got," Michael said, softly. "I told Amy I'd take *her* there. I'm sorry. It just sort of came out. I don't know why I said it. I just couldn't think of anything else."

"But you haven't got a ticket for her," said Callum. "And they've probably sold out by now."

"Well. . ." Michael hardly dared ask. "I was wondering. . .?"

"Oh no!" said Callum, firmly. "Definitely not. You're not having my ticket, Michael. No way!"

Three

They arrived at the Granville in Callum's battered old Mini, parked in a side street and raced to the foyer of the club to enquire if there were still any tickets left for the following evening.

"It depends how many you want," said the woman in the booking office. "We've only got three."

"We only need one," said a relieved Michael as he took out his wallet.

"We'll have two," Callum jumped in. He grinned at Michael. "I'm not playing gooseberry to you two. I'll have to bring someone . . . and you can pay for them."

Michael reluctantly paid for the two tickets, kept one for himself and handed the other to a beaming Callum.

"So who are you going to ask?" he said.

Callum shrugged. "I don't know. Perhaps I should ask Amy's friend, Hannah. Then we could go as a foursome."

Michael was delighted. "Hey, that's great, Callum. We'll have a laugh."

As they headed back towards the car, Callum was beginning to look serious. "I hope she won't get any ideas, though," he said. "I don't want her thinking I fancy her, or anything like that."

"She's very attractive, Callum," said Michael. "And she winked at you, don't forget." He paused. "She seems like a laugh."

By lunchtime the following day, a heavy storm had prevented the upper school from sunbathing on the amphitheatre steps.

"Not that it matters," Amy said dreamily, as she and Hannah lounged in their form room, half reading, half gazing out at the rain bouncing off the windows. "It wouldn't be the same walking down the steps, knowing he wasn't there."

"You've really got it bad, haven't you?" smiled Hannah. "I only hope he's not a let-down tonight. I can't believe you're going to the Granville with him. You *hate* the Granville. You swore you'd never go there again."

"I might get to like it," grinned Amy, "if I've got hunky Michael with his arm round me."

Callum popped his head into the year-eleven common room, saw the two girls and crossed to them. "Hi!" He dragged up a spare chair and sat opposite.

Amy and Hannah were surprised to see him. "Hi!" they replied in unison.

"We haven't really spoken, have we?" he said. "I'm Callum. But I'm sure you know that, already."

Amy smiled at him. "We *had* heard. Yes."

"So . . . I hear you're going to the Granville tonight with Michael," he said to Amy.

"That's right," Amy replied.

"She can't wait," interrupted Hannah. "She loves the Granville, don't you, Amy?"

Callum didn't look at Hannah. "Do you?" he asked Amy. "I do too. I've had loads of good times there."

"It'll be packed tonight," added Hannah.

Callum still didn't look at Hannah. He was suddenly struck by Amy's dark green eyes. She and Michael would certainly make a good couple. "I'm going too," he said. "I really like Decoy."

Hannah couldn't contain herself. "*You're* going? Not with Amy and Michael, surely?"

Amy nudged her friend with her elbow. "Hannah!" she reprimanded her. "He didn't say he was going with us."

"Oh, but I am," said Callum.

Amy looked horrified. Her first date with Michael, and his best friend would be tagging along.

Still Callum didn't address Hannah. He looked down at his shoes, attempting, but failing, to appear nonchalant. "I

27

thought we could go as a foursome," he said nervously. "You know . . . you and Michael and me and Hannah."

"Really?" gasped Hannah. "Oh, that would be fantastic."

"Er . . . yes," stammered Amy. "That would be really nice, Callum."

"I'm picking Michael up at quarter to eight," Callum went on. "And then we'll come and pick you two up at your place, Amy. Is that all right?"

"Yes," she said. "Perfect."

"Pick us up?" enquired Hannah. "You haven't got a car, have you?"

For the first time, Callum glanced in Hannah's direction. "Of course I've got a car," he replied. He stood and looked down at Amy, "So, see you tonight then," he said. And he left.

"Well! What about that?" said Amy. "You've been asked out on a date, Hannah." She laughed. "By the boy you've always called 'that tall one with the ginger hair'."

"He's quite nice, though, isn't he?" said Hannah. "He's quite good-looking really, when you get close up to him. And he's got great legs."

Amy laughed. "Great legs? *Long* legs, you mean."

"*And* he's got a car," sighed Hannah. "I've always wanted to go out with someone who's got a car."

"Aah. . ." Amy said, tongue in cheek, ". . .that's why you've suddenly decided he's quite nice. It's the car!"

Hannah giggled. "Of course it's not the car. It's *him*. I *like* him." She grabbed Amy's arm. "Hey! I hope it's a car with plenty of *leg* room." She shrieked with laughter. "I hope it's not a Mini!"

"You look really gorgeous," Hannah said as she and Amy sat side by side, staring into Amy's bedroom mirror while they put on their make-up.

"You too," replied Amy. "I think I prefer your hair up like that."

"I hope *he* does," grinned Hannah. "You don't think he's taking me along out of sympathy, do you?" she asked. "You don't think he felt sorry for me, because I was being left out?"

"Don't be ridiculous," replied Amy. "Anyway," she added, "would that bother you? You want to see Decoy. That's the whole point of the evening. It's not as though you fancy him or anything, is it?"

Hannah smiled at her through the mirror. "Well. . ."

Amy's eyes widened. "You *do*! You *do* fancy him!"

A car-horn sounded from the street outside and Hannah raced to the window to take a look. She stared open-mouthed and then turned back to Amy, with a glint in her eye. "They're here," she said. "In the *Mini*!"

The Granville was, as expected, packed. Michael managed to

grab a table in one of the crowded, dimly-lit alcoves and all four sat, looking out across the empty dance-floor.

"Not a lot of elbow room, is there?" Callum shouted above the DJ's over-amplified sound.

"It'll get better when people start dancing," Hannah replied, knowledgeably. "We'll probably have this alcove all to ourselves then. It's early yet."

"What time are Decoy on?" asked Amy.

Michael looked at his watch. "Not for ages. I'll get us some drinks."

They placed their orders and, as Michael squeezed through the crowd to get to the bar, Callum turned to Hannah. "Do you want to dance?" he asked her.

Hannah hesitated, not wanting to leave Amy sitting on her own. "Shall we wait till Michael gets back?" she said. "Anyway, I hate being the first on the dance-floor. I'll feel a bit braver when there are more people up there."

He smiled at her. "Yeah. Let's wait for Michael. We'll all dance together, eh?"

Hannah stared at him, examining his features: the spiky red hair, the strong Roman nose, and the broad jaw. Although he was far from being conventionally good-looking, he was, to Hannah's mind . . . extremely attractive. She was aware, however, that this date with him might be just a one-off; that he'd probably only asked her along to make up a foursome.

Michael eventually managed to struggle back through the crowd and put the drinks on the table.

"It wasn't too bad, actually," he said. "I thought I'd be ages."

Building up towards Decoy's imminent arrival, the DJ decided to play their latest hit single. The sound of *Get up and Dance* reverberated off the walls and, almost as one, the crowd surged towards the dance-floor.

"Shall we?" asked Michael, smiling at Amy.

"Why not?" She put her drink down and followed him on to the dance-floor.

Without speaking, Callum put his hand out to grip Hannah's.

She stood up. "I feel braver *now*," she giggled . . . and she pulled him to his feet.

When Decoy hit the stage, a little after eleven, the floor was crowded and the alcoves totally empty. The musicians lived up to their reputation of being one of the best of the new live bands and the crowd yelled and screamed for encore after encore.

Hannah had got completely wound up in the excitement, leaping up and down with the crowd, all shoulder to shoulder, hemmed in around the stage. Callum leaped up and down beside her, occasionally giving her a wide grin as they both sang along to Decoy's last top-forty hit.

Amy kept looking at her watch, knowing that she'd promised her parents she'd be home by midnight.

"Michael," she said finally. "I really must go. If you want to stay, then Hannah and I can get the bus."

"Don't be daft," he said. "Of course you're not getting the bus." He pushed his way towards the stage and tapped a sweating Callum on the shoulder, mouthing, "We're off. Are you coming?"

Callum looked disappointed, but grabbed Hannah's hand and pulled her through the crowd to where Amy stood.

"Sorry," said Amy. "But my mum'll panic if I'm not home soon."

Callum smiled at the beautiful blonde girl who Michael had his arm round. "No problem," he said. "Let's go."

As they left the club, the air hit them like a wet sponge, making their sweat-streaked faces feel cold and clammy.

"It was so hot in there," gasped Amy. "You'd have thought they'd have air-conditioning . . . especially during a hot summer like this."

"Not so hot tonight," said Callum as he began to cross the main road. "I think it's all changed after that storm."

"Too hot for an arm around you?" Michael whispered to Amy.

"Not too hot for *that*," she whispered back.

As Hannah followed Callum across the road, Michael

put both his arms around Amy's waist and pulled her towards him. They stood at the kerb, staring into each others' eyes.

"Have you had a good evening?" he asked her.

"Great, thank you. Have you?"

"I really like you, Amy," he said.

"Good," she smiled. "I'm glad. I like you too, Michael."

"So can we do it again?" he asked, a little tentatively.

"When?" she asked. She laughed, realizing she was sounding more than keen.

"I'll see you at lunchtime tomorrow," he said. "On the amphitheatre steps. And we'll arrange something, eh?"

"Supposing it's raining tomorrow?" she asked.

"Who cares about a bit of rain," he replied. "If you're there it'll be sunshine all the way."

They both laughed.

"You should be a poet," she said. "Or *not*."

He grinned. "Yeah. Writing crass comments on greetings cards."

They stopped laughing and stared, silently, at each other. He tightened his grip around her waist and pulled her even closer. Then, gently . . . very gently . . . he kissed her.

"Amy!" Hannah called from the other side of the road. "I thought you were worried about getting home?"

*

Callum huffed and puffed as he tried over and over again to start the car.

"What's wrong with it?" he said. "It's never done this before!"

Hannah sat in the front passenger seat, staring out through the windscreen. "Perhaps it's damp," she suggested. "After the storm."

"Don't be stupid!" he snapped. "It got us here, didn't it?"

Hannah was furious. "Don't talk to me like that, you great pillock! I was only trying to help!"

Callum was ashamed at his outburst. "Sorry," he said. "I didn't mean to sound. . ."

Michael leaned forward from the back seat, still holding Amy's hand. "I thought you were supposed to know all about cars, Callum," he said.

Amy looked at her watch. "I'm going to be so late," she said. She too leaned forward. "Look, I'm sorry, Callum, but I'm going to have to get the bus."

"Leave the car here, Callum," suggested Michael. "We'll come back for it tomorrow."

"I can't leave it here," sighed Callum. "It won't have any wheels left by the morning. You know what they're like around here." He turned to face Amy and Michael. "I'm sorry about this," he said. "It's ruined the evening."

"Of course it hasn't," Michael assured him. "It's not your fault."

"You can never trust old bangers like these," added Hannah, insensitively.

"You lot had better get the bus," said Callum. "I'll ring my dad and get him to come over. He'll sort it out. I'll see you all at school tomorrow."

Hannah had never before felt so unwelcome, even though Michael and Amy had engaged her in conversation throughout the bus journey home. She tried to avert her eyes every time Michael squeezed Amy's hand a little more tightly. She knew they wanted to be alone, but the rest of the bus was full. There was nowhere else to sit, except on one of the long seats . . . facing them. The walk home from the bus stop to the Belling Estate was even worse. It seemed endless to Hannah as the two of them strolled along, arm in arm beside her.

Finally, they reached Amy's gate.

"I'll see you tomorrow," Hannah said quickly as she began to walk off.

Amy stopped her. "Hannah! You're not going home on your own. Michael'll walk with you." She smiled at him. "Won't you, Michael?"

He tried to cover his disappointment. He wanted a few more minutes alone with her. He was hoping for a goodnight kiss. And so was she. But she also knew that her father was probably watching her every move from the landing window.

"Of course I'll walk you home, Hannah," he said.

He quickly kissed Amy on the cheek. "See you tomorrow," he said. "Come rain or shine."

Then he walked off across the Belling Estate with Hannah.

Four

Hannah strolled slowly past the tennis courts and down towards the amphitheatre. She knew that she wouldn't be welcomed by Amy and Michael, but she couldn't think what else to do.

She reached the top of the steps and saw her best friend, lying on her front. Michael lay beside her, with his arm around her. They were both engrossed in conversation. For a while she stood and stared at them. Then she turned and walked back into school . . . heading for the library.

"It's an exchange," Michael told Amy. "This guy from Spain will come over and live in my house. And I'll be living with his parents in Madrid. It should be fun."

"D'you think so?" asked Amy. "I wasn't that keen on Spain myself. I prefer France."

"Except when you're camping," he laughed.

"Not keen on camping. No." She laughed too.

"You've probably only seen the touristy Spain, though, haven't you?"

"Yes. Two weeks in Marbella."

"Me too," he told her. "But this time I'll see the *real* Spain. No English or German tourists. Just Spaniards. It's the best way to study the language."

"I wish *I* could speak a foreign language," she sighed. "I've never been very good at it."

"If you came with me you'd be speaking fluent Spanish in no time," he said.

She felt her heart flutter.

"Not that you could of course," he added, quickly. 'I don't think the Spanish family in Madrid would approve if I turned up with you in tow."

"I don't suppose they would," she replied softly.

He gently ran his fingers upwards . . . along the nape of her neck and then through the back of her blonde hair. "But it's a nice thought, isn't it?" he said.

"Very," she purred. She lifted her head to face him. "It's a pity you have to go away for so long," she said, plaintively. "Five weeks!"

"Yes," he replied. "I was really looking forward to it, but now I'm not so sure."

"Why's that?" she asked, although she understood exactly what he was implying.

"I think you know why," he said.

She closed her eyes and turned over, wrapping her arms around his broad back. And as he kissed her, she saw images of sun-drenched Spanish beaches and palm trees. She could almost feel the incoming tide gently lapping over their sand-and-salt-streaked bodies. And she wished, so much, that she could go with him.

He arrived at seven-thirty as arranged and found her ready to leave.

"Don't keep her out too late, Michael," Amy's mum demanded. "I know it's Saturday tomorrow, but it's still a twelve o'clock deadline, don't forget."

"Of course I won't," he replied, fully aware that he was charming Amy's mum with his dazzling smile. "We're only going into town for a walk. We'll be back well before midnight. I promise."

As they opened the front door, they were surprised to see Hannah standing there, about to ring the bell. She was holding a carrier bag.

"Oh. Sorry," said Hannah, looking embarrassed. "I didn't know you two were going out tonight. I just thought I'd bring round these CDs before I. . ."

Amy too was embarrassed. She didn't want to let Hannah down. They'd always gone out together on Friday evenings, ever since either of them could remember. "Oh sorry! I thought I said that Michael was calling for me tonight."

Hannah began to blush. "Yes, but I didn't think he'd be here quite so early, so. . ."

"We're only going for a walk," said Amy. "You can come with us if you like."

It was only a half-hearted gesture as all three of them were aware.

"Don't be silly," said Hannah. "Anyway, I'm supposed to be meeting someone later," she added as she handed Amy the carrier bag. "It's just that I had an hour to spare and so. . ." She turned to walk away, calling back over her shoulder, "I'll see you at school on Monday."

"I'll ring you in the morning," Amy called after her. "We'll arrange something for tomorrow night."

"OK!" Hannah replied and she raced off before her blushes became more obvious.

The park, on this long, hot summer's evening, was still open and Michael led Amy by the hand, along the gravel path towards the pond. They sat on the bench, watching the ducks being fed by an old woman carrying a crumpled paper bag filled with bread.

"Who do you think she's meeting?" asked Michael.

"Who? That old lady?" asked Amy.

Michael laughed. "No. Hannah. She said she was meeting someone later."

"No one," Amy assured him. "She just said that, because she was embarrassed." She sighed. "I do feel bad about it. We always go out together on Friday nights."

Michael put his arm around her and pulled her close to his side. She rested her head on his shoulder.

"You should've told me," he said. "You can't go letting her down like that. She *is* your best friend, Amy. We could've gone out tomorrow instead."

Amy sighed. "Yes. You're right. I hate the thought of hurting her."

Michael smiled. "Hey, you don't think she's meeting Callum, do you?"

"If only," replied Amy.

"Does she like him?" asked Michael.

"Yes. She says she thinks he's really attractive. What about *him*?" she enquired. "Does *he* like *her*?"

Michael shrugged. "He said he didn't fancy her," he replied. "But that was before we all went to the Granville." He pulled Amy closer to him. "They seemed to get on all right together, didn't they?"

"But hasn't he said anything about her?" she asked.

Michael felt guilty. He'd been so full of his own new-found romance with Amy, he hadn't even asked Callum about Hannah.

"Er . . . no," he said. "No, he hasn't mentioned her. Perhaps I should ask him how he feels about her."

Amy smiled. "Yes. Perhaps you should."

Earlier, having left Michael and Amy canoodling away their lunchtime, Hannah had gone to the library to write some letters. She was hoping to get a job to see her through the summer holidays, but so far none of the letters she'd written had received a reply. However, she was determined to keep trying. She wasn't surprised to find the library almost empty. It was such a beautiful day and she knew that anyone with any sense would be spending their lunchtime outside.

The only other person there, sitting at the long table near the door, nose in a book on car-mechanics, was Callum. At first she wondered if she should quietly disappear. She didn't want him to think that she was following him; that she was coming on too strong. Then she decided that she had every right to be here and if he didn't like the thought of her sitting with him, then he could always make some excuse and leave.

She deliberately sat right opposite him and took out her note-pad and pen. He didn't look up. He stared down at page 106, headlined: THE OIL FILTER. His hands covered his ears, blocking out any sound around him. He was totally engrossed. Hannah grinned mischievously. She picked up her pen and began to write:

Dear Callum,

This is not a love letter! I'm sitting opposite you now, staring at your ruggedly handsome face and wishing I could run my fingers through that beautiful red hair. This is not a love letter! I can just see those hairs peeping up over the top of your open-necked shirt and thinking how nice it would be if you looked up at me at this very moment with those sparkling brown eyes. This is not a love letter! As our two best friends seem to be totally in lerv (!) and not able to spend time with us any more, I thought we could maybe go out together somewhere. There! I bet you've never had an invitation like that from someone as beautiful as me. Take up the offer, or live to regret it!

Love, Hannah xxx

PS This is not a love letter.

PPS You've got lovely legs.

Fighting back the giggles, Hannah pushed the letter across the table towards Callum's textbook.

He didn't see it.

She pushed it further.

He still didn't react.

She sighed, picked up the letter and placed it down on top of page 106: THE OIL FILTER.

Callum stiffened and stared at the handwritten page in front of him. Without looking up, he slowly read the letter. Hannah watched the corners of his mouth turn up as he tried to suppress his laughter. Then, still not looking at her, he grappled in the top pocket of his jacket which was hanging over the back of his chair, and took out a pen. He turned over Hannah's letter and wrote on the back of it:

> *Dear admirer,*
> *Thank you for your letter. I'm glad you like my*
> *handsome face and red hair. And yes . . . you're right . . .*
> *my legs are rather nice. Let's meet tonight at eight-thirty*
> *outside McDonald's.*
> *From, Callum*
> *PS This is not a love letter!*

Still not looking at her, he pushed the letter back across the table.

Hannah picked it up, read it, packed her bag and began to leave the library. As she passed by the back of his chair, she playfully ran her hand over his hair. Just one stroke . . . and she was gone.

"Do you fancy a burger or something?" Michael asked Amy as they walked, hand in hand, through the town centre. "I've got some cash on me."

They reached McDonald's and Amy sat on a low wall outside the restaurant, which surrounded a tiny shrub-bed recently planted by the local council.

"I'll wait here," she said. "It's too nice to sit indoors."

As Michael left her to queue at the counter, Amy gazed up at the cloudless sky, just beginning to darken. She could see the crescent moon and the promise of a thousand stars which would soon appear. It was an awesome night, a gentle breeze now weakening the stifling heat of the day and, for the first time, it really hit her that in just a few weeks' time, Michael could be staring up at this very moon and these very same stars, although he'd be a thousand miles away.

Her feelings began to frighten her. She knew it couldn't be love. Not yet. Hadn't her mother told her, many times, that love takes time to grow; that there was no such thing as love at first sight. And Amy realized that she didn't *know* Michael at all. There was so much to learn about him but, unfortunately, they didn't have time to spare. Soon he'd be leaving and when he returned, things would be so different. She'd be about to start college and he'd be returning to Melthorn High.

From that moment, she determined to make the most of the next few weeks; to find out if he really was the boy she hoped he was . . . and if he was . . . then a five-week absence shouldn't make any difference to the way they felt about each other. Five weeks! Her stomach lurched. How would she bear it?

She gazed through the restaurant window and saw him slowly easing forward in the queue, his blond hair appearing almost white in the bright lights above him. And then her eye caught the diners on the corner table and she gasped, audibly. She could hardly believe it. Callum and Hannah, chatting away to each other, smiling, laughing over their burgers and fries. She stood and raced into the restaurant, tugging at Michael's arm and pointing in Callum and Hannah's direction.

Michael smiled broadly. "Well, well, well," he said. "Would you believe it. There's *my* best friend . . . with *your* best friend. Dating. Secretly."

Amy crossed to their table and sat down. They both looked at her, rather nervously.

Amy smiled. "You didn't tell me you two were out on a date tonight."

"We're not," Hannah replied quickly. "We're just friends," she added, sounding peculiarly guilty. "It's not a date. Not a *real* date. Is it, Callum?"

His reply surprised her. "Course it's a real date. Why?" he asked her, with a mischievous grin. "Are you ashamed to be seen with me or something?"

Hannah laughed. "No. It's just. . ."

46

Callum reached forward and took Hannah's hand. "We're going to the Granville later," he informed Amy.

"Are we?" asked a shocked Hannah.

"You two can come with us if you want to," added Callum.

"I can't," replied Amy. "I've promised to be back before twelve and you know what Friday nights are like at the Granville. Nothing gets started till eleven-thirty."

Michael arrived at the table with a tray of burgers, fries and coffee. "Hi, you two!" he said. "What a surprise."

"Callum and Hannah want us to go to the Granville with them," Amy told him, "but I can't."

"Oh. Shame," said Michael. "Who's on tonight?"

"It doesn't stop *you* going, Michael," Amy said.

Michael gripped her hand. "And why would I want to go without you?"

"Are *we* still going?" Hannah asked Callum, trying to sound cool, trying to pretend it didn't really bother her if they went or not.

Callum looked at her in surprise. "Of course we are. Don't you want to?"

"Yes. Yes, course I do," stammered Hannah. "But it's just the two of us and. . ."

"Have you finished stuffing your face?" Callum interrupted her.

Hannah laughed. "Yes."

"Then let's go," he said as he reached out for her hand.

He and Hannah stood up.

"What are you two doing tomorrow?" Callum asked Michael and Amy.

They looked at him, blankly.

"Nothing," said Michael.

"Nothing. Why?" Amy added.

"So how about a picnic in the country? The four of us. I can take us in the car."

"In that Mini?" gasped Hannah. "Are you sure?"

"That would be great," said Michael.

"Fantastic," added Amy.

"Right!" Callum grinned. "If you all bring some food and drink, I'll pick you up at Amy's about ten."

"Are we really going in that Mini?" asked Hannah, her eyes twinkling. She looked at Amy and grinned. "Not a lot of leg room, is there?"

Callum smiled. "I hope you're not referring to *my* legs," he said. "I thought you liked my legs, Hannah." He kissed her on the cheek, which surprised everybody, including Hannah. Then he turned to Michael and Amy, announcing in a mock whisper, "Hannah really likes my legs."

Hannah blushed as Callum led her to the door, leaving their stunned friends gazing after them.

Five

"I think it was down here somewhere," announced Callum as he carefully manoeuvred the battered Mini along a pot-holed country lane. "Mind you, I haven't been here since I was about five years old, so I might've got it wrong."

Hannah bumped up and down in the seat beside him. "Five years old!" she groaned. "Callum! You'll never remember where it is! Anyway, I still can't understand why we're going to somewhere called Bluebell Wood," she added. "There's not going to be many bluebells about in July."

"There won't be *any*," said Amy from the back seat. Sweat was trickling down her face and she leaned forward trying to get some air from Hannah's open window.

Callum tutted. "It's not called Bluebell Wood," he explained. "*We* called it Bluebell Wood when we were kids."

"That's because it was full of bluebells, I expect," said

49

Michael, somewhat sarcastically.

"That's right," replied Callum. "We used to come here in the spring." He looked through his mirror and saw Michael and Amy's sweat-streaked faces. "I'm sorry," he said. "Perhaps this wasn't a good idea after all. I wasn't expecting it to be *quite* so hot today."

"It's not your fault, Callum," said Michael. "It's a great idea. It's just that we're a bit cramped."

Even though they were all wearing just shorts and T-shirts, they'd spent more than two hours in extreme discomfort. And although Callum had made such an effort to please, being squeezed into his tin can of a car on such a hot, sticky day, had made them all feel a little bit irritable.

Callum suddenly skidded the car to a halt. A white signpost pointed the way to Skegly and to Chatsfield.

"I think it's Skegly we want," he said. "But then, I might be wrong. It could be Chatsfield."

"Chatsfield sounds nicer," smiled Hannah. "Let's go to Chatsfield."

Callum took the right fork, heading for Skegly.

"Or, of course, we could always go to Skegly," she giggled.

The lane began to narrow, winding its way through the vibrant yellow fields of rape, before rising upwards past picture-book green fields scattered with poppies and unidentifiable wild flowers.

Hannah sighed and clutched Callum's bare knee. "Better than the park, Callum," she said.

Amy agreed. "It's beautiful, Callum. Bluebells or no bluebells."

Callum suddenly cried out like a small boy, "This is it! I'm sure this is it." He stopped the car at the side of a crumbling stile, leaped out . . . and gazed open-mouthed across the sheep-dotted field beyond. "This brings back memories," he sighed.

The others tumbled out after him, gasping for air, their clothes sticking to them.

"It's over there," explained Callum. "On the other side of this field. Bluebell Wood."

"Without bluebells," grinned Hannah.

"We can't just leave the car here," said Michael. "Nothing can get by."

"If I remember right, there's a lay-by further up the hill," said Callum. "Let's unload the picnic and you lot can wait here while I go and park."

Armed with carrier bags, they crossed the field and headed for the trees on the other side. It was a relief to be in the shade, though the wood was not as inviting as they'd all hoped. The recent storms had flattened much of it . . . and the fallen trunks, some thankfully sprouting signs of new life, had blocked the way through to where Callum, as a small

51

boy, used to picnic with his parents.

"What a shame," he said as they climbed over fallen oaks and beeches, brushing aside clinging ivy and other creepers. "It's been totally destroyed."

"And not a bluebell in sight," said Hannah, trying to lighten Callum's disappointment.

They struggled onwards, encouraged by Callum's calls from ahead, until the wood finally came to an end and opened out on to rolling green hills, littered with the yellows and whites of a thousand buttercups and daisies.

The sun, now a little watery, felt wonderful and they quickly found a perfect picnic spot. They took off their shoes and spread out their picnic on the white sheet which Amy had borrowed from her mother's airing cupboard.

As the others began to eat, Michael took off his shirt and lay on his stomach, feeling the warm rays settling between his shoulder blades. The gold chain around his neck glinted in the sunlight and Amy leaned over and gently fingered it. "I haven't seen this before," she said. "Is it new?"

Michael immediately sat up and helped himself to a sandwich. "Yes. Do you like it?" he asked.

"I've got one almost the same," she replied. "See?" She pulled out the chain, hidden under her shirt.

Michael didn't look at it. There was no need to. He'd seen it when they'd been lying on the steps together. And that's when the idea had struck him.

"Michael?" she asked, wondering why he hadn't responded.

"I know," he said, dismissively, as he reached out for a can of Coke. "They're very similar."

Hannah suddenly gasped. On the far side of the field, she could see something moving towards them. She raised her hand, shielding her eyes from the sun, and tried to make out the approaching mass.

"Callum? What's that?" she asked.

Callum stared and laughed. "Cows," he said. "They're coming to find out what we're doing."

They all turned to look.

"I hope you're right, Callum," said Amy. "I hope they're not bulls."

"They're bullocks," said Michael. "They won't hurt you. They're just curious."

The herd slowly approached and stopped a few metres away, gazing at the picnickers.

Hannah froze. "I don't like it," she said. "They look as though they're going to charge."

"I hope they don't charge much," said Callum. "I've only got fifty pence on me."

The others laughed.

Callum flung his arms around Hannah's neck. "They won't

hurt you while I'm around," he said with a smile. "Because I'm brave . . . and I'm strong . . . and I'm. . ." He suddenly whisked everything off the white sheet and stood, holding it up like a matador's cloak towards the staring herd. "*Olé!*" he yelled, as he stamped his feet and twirled around with the cloth, flapping it up and down. "Come on, you wild beasts! Do your worst!"

Michael stared at him, incredulously. "He'll never grow up," he said with a smile.

"You'll get a shock if one of them *does* actually charge," said Amy.

The bullocks, looking bored, slowly began to turn and amble away.

"There!" laughed Callum. "They know who's boss around here."

"Perhaps you ought to give Michael a lesson in bullfighting," suggested Hannah. "He may need it in Spain if he comes across any of those wild, black bulls over there."

Amy suddenly looked gloomy. She'd managed for a few hours to push the fact aside that Michael would soon be leaving. Hannah saw the look on her face and rather than draw attention to it, she quickly tried to change the subject. "So what about this after-lunch surprise you've got for us, Callum?" she said. "What is it?"

He playfully grabbed her around the neck again and dragged her backwards until she was lying flat out on the grass. She screamed and giggled.

"If I told you, then it wouldn't be a surprise, would it?" he said. He leaned across her, pinning her arms by her side . . . and then quickly kissed her, before releasing her. "Was that surprise enough for you?" he asked.

She sat up, laughing. "Call that a surprise?" she said, pretending to wipe away his kiss on the back of her hand. "I hope it's a bit better than that."

Having packed the picnic things into the carrier bags, they continued the walk across the field, heading for what Callum called his big surprise. The sun had now regained its full power and Michael had put his T-shirt back on. He wanted his body to retain its golden tan. He didn't want to burn and peel.

A short trek through another tiny wood brought them out on to a cliff-edge and they all beamed when they saw the sea ahead of them.

"I had no idea we were this close to the coast," said Amy.

"That's why I asked you not to look at the map," Callum informed them. "This is the surprise. An after-lunch swim."

A steep path led them down, through banks of nettles, bustling with butterflies, to a tiny shingle beach.

"We used to come here in the spring," said Callum, "But it was too cold to swim. I don't think anyone else knows it exists."

"It's fantastic," sighed Amy as she gazed longingly at the tiny waves lapping gently on to the shore. "What a pity we haven't brought our swimming things."

"Who needs them!" yelped Michael as he kicked off his trainers, peeled off his T-shirt and raced to the water's edge. Callum did the same, chasing after him.

"You'll get your shorts wet!" called Hannah as she watched them run straight into the sea.

"They'll dry again!" Callum called back.

Hannah looked at Amy and smiled. Amy returned the smile. Then, dropping the carrier bags on to the shingle, both girls raced down to the sea and, fully clothed, they leaped into the water.

Exhausted, they lay back on the shingle, feeling their wet clothes quickly being dried out by the sun. Amy, worried about getting burnt on this sun-trap of a beach, used one corner of the picnic sheet to lay across her face as a protective shield. Michael lay beside her, one arm wrapped around her, wishing they could stay like this for ever. Further along the beach they could hear Hannah's squeals of delight as she and Callum searched the rock pools for tiny crabs and shrimp.

"I had a letter today," Michael mumbled, his face down in the shingle.

Amy removed the sheet from her face. "Oh?"

"From Spain."

"Oh." She sighed. "From the family you're staying with?"

"Sort of. Actually, it's from their son. My exchange partner."

"Really? Does he sound OK?" she asked.

"Yes. He sounds quite nice," Michael said. He too sighed. "He sent a photo."

"And?"

"Frightened me a bit," he said. "He's really good-looking."

Amy sat up, looking down at Michael. He turned over on to his back and gazed up at her. "He looks like a film star."

"What, like Michael Caine, you mean?" she laughed.

"More like Brad Pitt," he replied, grimacing.

"So, what's the problem?" she asked. "You won't even meet him, will you?"

"Briefly," he said. "In Madrid. You'll meet him here."

"Me? Why should *I* meet him?" She was surprised.

"Because I was hoping you'd look after him, maybe. Take him around and show him some typically English places. Would you?"

"Of course I will. If you want me to," she replied.

He grinned up at her. "I *did* want you to. But now I've seen his picture, I'm not so sure."

"You sound jealous," she said.

"I would be," he replied. "If I thought you'd fancy him."

She gently ran her finger across his forehead. "That dark Mediterranean look doesn't appeal to me," she replied, honestly. "I go for blonds."

"You haven't seen him, Amy!"

"He couldn't possibly be as gorgeous as you, Michael," she said.

He reached up and pushed her hair away from her eyes. Then he slowly pulled her down towards him. She lay her head on his chest, listening to the beating of his heart, gently stroking up and down his side with her fingertips.

"Look what we've found!" yelled Hannah from above them. They felt her shadow fall across them, blocking out the sun. Michael and Amy sat up, trying not to show their irritation at being disturbed. Callum stood beside Hannah, holding out his hand.

"It's a gold cross!" said Hannah, excitedly. "From a chain. Someone must've lost it when they went swimming."

"I thought you said no one else comes here, Callum?" asked Michael.

Callum shrugged. "Perhaps it got washed up from another beach."

"Maybe it was lost on a beach abroad somewhere," suggested Amy. "It could've been washed here from France." She grinned. "Australia even. Who knows?"

"Or Spain," Callum said, without thinking. "You could take

it over with you when you go, Michael . . . and ask around. See if it belongs to anyone." He laughed loudly. "Here," he said as he handed it to Michael.

Michael refused to take it. "You found it," he said. "You keep it."

Callum insisted. "I haven't got a chain to put it on," he said. "Put it on *yours*," he added. "Then when you're away it'll remind you of the day we all spent here."

Michael silently took the cross. "Thanks, Callum," he said, somewhat sadly. "I will."

They sat on the stile, carrier bags at their feet, looking back across the sheep-inhabited field, waiting for Callum to bring the car from the lay-by.

"What a fantastic day," sighed Amy.

"And it didn't really matter about the bluebells, did it?" laughed Hannah.

Michael looked along the road and saw Callum strolling despondently towards them. "Oh-oh," he said. "Something's wrong."

"Oh no," said Hannah. "Don't say he can't start the car."

She looked at her watch. It was six o'clock. "My parents were expecting me home for tea. I'm late as it is!"

Callum reached them and sighed, resignedly. "Sorry," he said. "I can't start the car."

Six

With the Mini's bonnet propped open, Callum unsuccessfully fiddled around with the engine until he had oil up to his elbows. The others stood around the car impatiently, hoping that he'd soon find the fault and that they could all set off for home.

"I'd help if I could," said Michael. "But I know nothing about cars, Callum. I'm sorry."

Hannah looked at her watch and tutted. "My dad'll go mad," she said.

Callum looked up, helplessly, from the engine. "It's no good," he sighed. "I can't see what's wrong with it."

"Could it be the oil filter?" Hannah asked, haughtily.

"I think we ought to try to get to a phone-box," said Amy. "We can call the AA or something, can't we?"

Callum shrugged. "I'm not a member."

"What about your dad?" suggested Michael. "He'll come and help, surely."

Callum climbed back into the Mini, picked up an oily rag and began to wipe his hands. "Hannah and I will go and see if we can find a phone-box," he said. He looked up at Michael and Amy from the car's opened door. "You two may as well stay here. It's pointless us all going." He leaped out from the car and put his hand out to take Hannah's. "Come on," he said.

Hannah backed away from him, grimacing at his oil-stained fingers. "I'll come with you," she said with a half-smile, "but I'm not holding that filthy hand."

Callum held up both his palms to show her just how ingrained the oil was. Then he began to approach her, grinning.

"You dare," she warned him as she started to run backwards.

He suddenly leaped towards her, reaching out for her hair with his fingers. Hannah screamed and then giggled as she turned and began to run along the country lane away from him. Callum chased after her, whooping and yelling. Michael and Amy watched the pair until they became two laughing and screaming dots in the distance.

"He'll never grow up," said Michael as he took Amy's arm.

"And neither will she," smiled Amy. "They're perfect for each other."

They strolled back to the stile and Michael climbed over it. Amy followed him, carrier bag in hand.

"We may as well make ourselves comfortable," he said. "They could be hours." He took the bag from Amy and reached inside it for the white sheet, which he spread out on the grass, carefully smoothing away all the wrinkles. Then he lay on his back and gently pulled Amy down beside him. She lay, silently, her arm across his chest, listening to his low breathing.

"Comfy?" he whispered.

"Very," she replied. She cuddled up close and shut her eyes, feeling the warmth of the late afternoon sun on her cheeks.

For minutes they said nothing, though both their heads were teeming with thoughts. She wondered if he would be able to read her mind; those thoughts and dreams of hers being so graphic. He hoped *she* couldn't read *his*.

Finally he spoke, keeping his eyes closed, not turning to her. "Have you been out with a lot of guys?"

"A few," she said. "But not like this. I've never *felt* like this."

He was silent.

"What about you?" she asked.

"Me?"

"Have you ever been this close to someone?" She was sure of the answer. Someone like *him*? Someone as good-looking as *him*? Of course he'd been out with other girls. Lots of them. And been as close as this. Closer than this. She was sure.

"No," he said. "Never."

She opened her eyes and looked at his tightly shut lids, examining their blond lashes and the bronzed, broad brow above them, slightly furrowed in consternation.

"Never?"

"Never."

"But you've had loads of girlfriends?"

"No."

"Of course you have," she said. "You must've been out with lots of girls."

"I've never been out with anyone," he said, worried that his naivety might put her off him completely.

"Really?" She was amazed.

He opened his eyes and turned his head to look at her. "Really."

"But you must have had girls throwing themselves at you," she said.

He grinned, shyly. "What's that got to do with it?" he asked.

She leaned up on one elbow, staring at him in disbelief. "Are you saying that I'm the first person you've ever been out with?"

"Yes." He gulped, turned his head away from her and closed his eyes again. "Does that worry you?"

63

She put her head on his chest and sighed, "Not at all."

"So you'll have to be gentle with me," he smiled.

She too smiled. "I'll be *very* gentle with you, Michael."

"With my heart, I mean," he added. "Don't break it, will you?"

She sighed deeply, though she felt there was no need for a reply.

"Night-night," he said softly.

She giggled. "Night-night."

Hannah and Callum had walked for miles, trying to find a call-box; Hannah constantly looking up at the sky, watching the light gradually fading.

"It'll be dark soon, Callum," she said, fearfully. "Suppose we can't find our way back to the car? We've got to find a phone soon."

Callum too was worried, but his reply came out as irritation. "What do you want me to do? Conjure up a call-box from thin air?"

Hannah smiled up at him, childlike. "You could *try*," she pleaded, softly. "For *me*."

He laughed. "Right," he said. "Here goes." He closed his eyes and pretended to wish. Then he opened them. "Done it!" he said with a grin. "For *you*."

As they turned the next corner and passed the sign for

Chatsfield, Hannah's mouth dropped open. A call-box was just ahead of them.

"How did you do that?" she asked.

He put his arm round her. "Magic," he replied.

Michael deftly unclipped his gold chain and removed it. He threaded it through the loop on the small cross which Callum had given him and held it up for Amy to see.

"It looks really good," she said. "Here," she took the chain and placed it around Michael's neck, refastening the catch.

"A gold cross," said Michael. "Should go down well in a Catholic country like Spain."

Amy stood and crossed to the stile. "It's getting cold." She shivered.

"And dark," added Michael. "Any sign of them?" he asked as he pushed the cross and chain inside his T-shirt.

Amy looked along the country lane for Hannah and Callum. "No."

"They've been gone for ages," said Michael. "I hope they haven't got lost. Surely they've found a phone-box by now?" He stood and gathered up the sheet, pushing it into the carrier bag. "Perhaps we should go and sit in the car. It'll be warmer."

"There they are!" Amy suddenly yelled. Far off, in the gloom, she could see two tiny figures approaching. She leaped

65

over the stile and ran along the lane towards them. "Where have you been?" she yelled.

Hannah laughed. "If we'd had to walk any further we'd have been home! There would've been no need to find a phone."

"But you did find one?" Amy asked, hopefully.

"Yes," said Hannah. "And I've rung your mum too, so she knows exactly what's going on."

"And my dad's on his way with his pick-up truck," added Callum. "But it'll probably take him a couple of hours."

As they reached the stile, Michael was leaning nonchalantly against it. "What kept you?" he asked, coolly. "I thought you'd deserted us for good."

"We'll have to wait in the car," said Amy. "It's getting chilly."

Callum grinned. "I've got a better idea. Let's get some sticks together before it gets dark."

"What? And build a fire?" asked Hannah with childlike excitement in her eyes.

Amy sneered at the idea. "And rub two sticks together to light it, I suppose?"

"Don't be daft," laughed Callum. "I've got a box of matches in the car."

"I'm starving," said Hannah, as the four of them sat around the tiny fire which was spitting and crackling under the

66

moonlit sky. "I suppose it's because bonfires remind me of baked potatoes."

They all looked at her quizzically.

"Dad always cooked baked potatoes in the bonfire on fireworks night," she explained. "The thought of it made me feel hungry."

Callum put his arm around her. "I'm hungry too," he grinned. "Hungry for love."

She giggled and pushed him away, affectionately. "You could go and catch one of those sheep, Callum," she said. "We could have roast lamb."

"Or one of those bullocks," added Michael. "A nice rump steak."

"I'm not going anywhere," said Callum. "I'm staying here . . . with my love." He laughed and once again wrapped his arm round Hannah. This time she didn't push him away.

"It *is* sort of romantic, isn't it?" sighed Amy as she put her hand on Michael's leg. "Sitting under the stars, around a camp-fire." A chill ran down her spine. "I don't suppose we'll ever do this again."

Michael gripped her hand. "Of course we will," he said, softly. "When I get back from Spain, the first thing we'll do is come back here and build a fire. Just like this."

"Let's make it a pact," said Callum seriously. "We'll all come back here to celebrate your return home."

"But it'll be autumn by then," said Hannah, thoughtlessly spoiling the dream. "It'll be cold and wet. It won't be like this."

The others fell silent.

"Have I said something wrong?" asked Hannah.

"No, you're right," agreed Amy. "Everything will have changed by then. Winter'll be coming. I'll be at college and you lot will still be at school. It'll never be the same again."

"Then we ought to make the most of it *now*," said Michael. He gently ran his fingers through Amy's hair before leaning forward and kissing her. She responded to his kiss, wrapping her arms around him and running her fingers up and down his back.

"Well?" Hannah asked Callum. "Follow my leader?"

Callum laughed. "Follow my leader!" he replied as he gripped Hannah tightly in his arms and kissed her.

And as the fire crackled and burned more brightly, shooting tiny sparks towards the star-littered sky, the two couples, lost in their euphoria, were unaware of the pick-up truck slowly heading along the lane towards them.

Seven

Hannah arrived early at school to find Amy in the North Cloakroom, staring desolately through the domed window towards the main gates.

"So, the big day's arrived then," said Hannah. "I thought it'd never get here."

It was the last day of term. The end of Amy's school life. And it felt even worse than she could possibly have imagined. Not only was she going to leave all her friends behind her; she now had to face the fact that she was going to be separated from Michael. They'd had such a short time together and just when everything seemed to be perfect, they were about to be torn apart. Even the weather had decided to be unkind on their last day together. After weeks of glorious sunshine, today it was drizzling, which meant they wouldn't be able to spend their last lunchtime outside on the steps of the amphitheatre.

"Hasn't he come yet?" asked Hannah as she watched the

early arrivals ambling through the gates. "I'd have thought he'd have been here really early today. After all, you haven't got long together, have you?"

Amy felt the lump tightening in her throat; the knot of sadness which was preventing her from replying to Hannah's questions.

Hannah saw the pained expression on her best friend's face and she gently placed an arm round her shoulder. "He'll be here soon," she said. "Don't panic."

A group of year-eleven school-leavers suddenly raced through the gates, whooping loudly. Some of them couldn't wait to say their goodbyes and Hannah wondered if there'd be the usual after-school hurling of flour bombs and eggs which, during yesterday's main assembly, the Head had strictly forbidden.

"There you are," said a voice from behind them. Hannah turned to see Callum grinning at them. "We've been here for ages," he said. "I thought we'd arranged to meet in the common room."

"Is Michael here?" asked Amy.

"Yes," replied Callum. "He's getting a bit worried, wondering why you haven't turned up."

Amy smiled. "Thanks." She immediately headed towards the common room.

Hannah began to follow, her, but Callum quickly grabbed her arm. "Where are you going?" he asked.

"Don't you want to go to the common room, too?" she asked, surprised.

Callum winked at her and took her hand, leading her towards the library. "Let's leave them on their own for a while, eh?"

Hannah immediately realized how insensitive she'd been. "Oh, yes. Of course," she smiled.

"It's not going to be easy for them today," explained Callum. "He's off to Spain this evening and who knows what'll happen after that?"

"He'll be back in five weeks," said Hannah. "It's not long." She paused, thinking on what she'd just said. "No. It *is* long," she added. "I wouldn't like it if *you* were going away for five weeks."

"And let's face it," said Callum, seriously, "he may decide he likes it out there. He might meet someone else and decide to stay."

"He can't," replied Hannah. "He's coming back to take his exams."

Callum shrugged. "All I'm saying is, you never know. They've got to make the most of today."

They walked into the library and both of them automatically sat at the table where they'd first passed notes to each other.

"Anyway, here's the good news," grinned Hannah. "I've got a summer job."

She expected Callum to react favourably. He didn't.

"Oh!" he said, gloomily. "What sort of job?"

"McDonald's," she informed him.

"Oh."

"I really need it, Callum," she said. "I haven't got any money at all. I thought you'd be pleased for me."

"I'm just being selfish," he said softly. "I was looking forward to spending the holiday with you. I wanted to go to the coast and stuff."

"I'll have some days off," she said quickly. "And I'm not working every evening."

He reached out for her hand and forced a smile. "Well, that's all right, then."

Michael was careful how he answered Amy's question.

"Well, yes, I *am* looking forward to it. I've always wanted to go to Spain. But I'm all mixed up inside."

"Me too," she said.

"I'll write every day," he promised. He paused. "I wish you were coming with me."

Her eyes filled with tears and she bit hard on her lip. "How would you get any studying done, if I was there?" she said. "You've got to speak Spanish all the time. That's why you're going. If we were both there, we'd be chatting away in English."

"Yes. I know you're right," he said. "It's just so. . ."

"As long as you don't spend all your time talking to some beautiful Spanish girl," she said, trying to smile through her tears.

"And talking of beautiful Spanish people," grinned Michael, "look at this." He reached into his bag for an envelope which he handed to Amy.

She opened it and took out a photo.

"Is this him?" she asked. "The Spanish boy?"

"Pedro. Yes. Well? What do you think?"

She studied the picture. The boy was extremely good-looking, as Michael had said, with a strong jaw and huge dark eyes and long black lashes. His hair, cut very short, was jet-black and his smile dazzled through his tanned skin.

"Wow! Ugly, isn't he?" laughed Amy.

"You can see why I was worried, can't you?" said Michael.

"What have you got to worry about?" she asked seriously, as she put the photo back into the envelope. "Yes. He's pretty gorgeous. But not as gorgeous as you."

"Really?"

She leaned forward and kissed him. "Really. There's no one else for me, Michael. There couldn't be. I love you."

These were the words he was waiting for; the words he was hoping she'd say on their last day together. He stood up and lifted her from her chair, wrapping his arms round her and pulling her tightly towards him.

"I love you too, Amy," he said. "I really do."

By lunchtime, the drizzle had turned to heavy rain and Amy was really disappointed. Had she realized yesterday, that what she'd believed to be her *penultimate* lunchtime on the steps with Michael, would turn out to be her *last*, then she would have relished the time even more. But, through a sudden change in the weather, it suddenly occurred to her that she'd already spent her last day on the steps, lying beside him, their arms wrapped around each other. It would never . . . *could* never, happen again. Not there! Not on the steps.

"Don't be daft," said Hannah as she and Amy entered the Central Hall to join the dozens of school-leavers all autographing each others' shirts. "Of course you won't be cuddling up to him on the steps again, but does it really matter *where* you do it?"

"No, I suppose not," replied Amy. "It's just full of great memories, that's all. It's where it all started."

"Then you'll have to keep those memories in your head," Hannah wisely lectured her. "You'll never forget those days on the steps . . . just as I'll never forget the library."

"The library?" Amy was curious.

Hannah laughed. "Never mind." She took out her pen. "Here, let me be the first to sign your shirt."

Callum and Michael waited at the top of the Central Hall stairs, not wishing to get involved with the tearful girls and the *seemingly* cheerful boys, who'd all suddenly realized that their school days were over. This was it!

"I'm going to really miss her, Callum," Michael said, flatly. "I don't know how I'm going to cope when the time comes to say goodbye."

"Is she going to the airport with you?" asked Callum.

"Yes. Unfortunately."

"Don't you want her to?"

"I *did* want her to," Michael explained. "It was my suggestion. My parents are working late, so they won't be there. And I thought it would be really great for us to spend a couple of hours together before I leave. But now, I'm not so sure it's a good idea. It's going to be very difficult."

"Hannah and I can come too, if you want," said Callum. "Then Amy won't be left alone when you go through the boarding gate."

"*Would* you?" asked Michael.

Callum smiled. "I'm sure you'd do the same for me."

"Look after her for me while I'm away," added Michael. "Don't let her be lonely, will you?"

"Hannah and I'll keep our beady eyes on her," said Callum. "Don't you worry about that."

Beaming, Amy ran up the steps towards the boys, followed by a giggling Hannah.

"Look at the state of *her*!" exclaimed Hannah.

Amy's white blouse was covered in signatures, the biggest of which, in green ink, was Hannah's.

Amy handed a pen to Callum. "Your turn," she said.

Callum signed his name on a white space on Amy's shoulder. "Treasure this," he laughed. "I might be famous one day and this'll be worth a fortune."

Hannah grinned and tutted. "Famous for *what*?"

Amy handed the pen to Michael.

"I'm not signing it," said Michael, firmly.

Amy looked disappointed. "Why?"

"Because all these signatures are from people you'll drift away from. Eventually. Most of them, you'll never see again after today. But as we're going to spend the rest of our lives together. . ."

Hannah looked at Callum. "Aaah! Why can't you say romantic things like that?" she asked with a twinkle in her eye.

"Because I'm not as wet as him," grinned Callum. "I'm a *real* man."

Michael laughed. "Are you sure?"

Hannah giggled. "Shall I tell you what he said to me yesterday? Bless him."

Callum began to blush. "You dare!" he said.

Hannah shrieked with laughter and took his hand. "Come on, lover boy," she said. "Let's go for a walk in the rain and leave these two alone."

"But I can't come to the airport, Callum," said Hannah, in despair. She stood in the puddle-filled playground, looking down at her feet. "I've got my training session at McDonald's tonight."

Callum was shocked. "I didn't think you'd be starting straight away."

"I'm sorry," said Hannah. "You'll have to go on your own. I can meet you both afterwards. About ten?"

Callum shook his head. "The flight isn't till nine-thirty. We won't be back here till gone eleven."

"Well, what can I do?" asked Hannah. "I can't take time off, can I? It's my first evening. If I say I've got to go early, I'll be sacked before I've even started."

Callum shrugged. "Don't worry. I'll look after her. I'm quite good at comforting maidens in distress."

Hannah looked a little concerned. "Just so long as you don't comfort her too much," she said.

Callum was annoyed, and hurt, at the suggestion. "What's that supposed to mean?"

"Nothing," Hannah replied softly. "Sorry. That was stupid of me."

"Yes. It was," Callum said, harshly. "Michael asked me . . . *us* . . . to look after her. And if you're not there. . ."

"I said I'm sorry," said Hannah. She grabbed Callum's hand. "Please. Don't let's argue. Not today."

"I'll go and wait in the coffee shop," said Callum as he stood with Michael and Amy at the gate to the departure lounge. He shook Michael's hand. "Have a great time, mate," he said. "And don't do anything I wouldn't do."

Michael affectionately slapped him on the back. "I'll see you in five weeks, Callum. Look after her, eh?"

"Trust me," replied Callum, with a grin. "Come and find me in the coffee shop when you're ready, Amy," he added. And he left.

Michael clutched Amy tighter than he'd ever done. "I don't want to go," he said. "All the excitement has disappeared. I just want to stay here with you."

She put her hand into her coat pocket and pulled out a small, purple envelope. "Here," she said. "I've written to you already and you haven't left the ground yet." She smiled. "It's the first of many. Hopefully."

He took the envelope and put it into his pocket. "A love letter?" he grinned.

"Maybe," she said. "Maybe not."

"I should've written you one, shouldn't I?" he said.

"Haven't you?" she asked, not at all surprised that he hadn't.

"Maybe," he said. "Maybe not."

They kissed. And both felt the tingle that surged through their bodies, now entwined as one.

"If I'm going to go, then I'd better go now," he said. "If I wait any longer, I might just change my mind."

She was determined not to cry. She wanted to look good for him as he turned to wave his last goodbye. No tears. No ugliness. She smiled. "I'll miss you," she said.

"I love you, Amy," he replied and he picked up his hand luggage and walked towards passport control.

She waited for him to turn back at the gate. He didn't. He couldn't. He didn't want her to see him looking so distressed. He walked swiftly through the gate and disappeared from view.

Amy gave one involuntary sob. She now knew what people meant by "a breaking heart". Hers was aching. A dull pain in her chest, like no other she'd ever felt. It's only five weeks, she thought. Only five weeks. Five weeks? Five long, painful weeks. She turned and headed for the coffee shop, where Callum was waiting. And there she fell into his open arms, laying her head on his chest and bursting into the tears which had been promising to flow for hours.

"Oh, Callum," she sobbed. "I can't bear it."

He gently stroked her hair. "He'll be back before you realize he's gone," he said, trying his best to comfort her. He took out a brown envelope from his pocket and handed it to her. "He told me to give you this," he said.

She stared at it. "What is it?"

He smiled. "How should *I* know? A love letter, probably."

She quickly tore open the envelope and took out the letter and the rest of its contents. The message on the letter was simple. "This'll keep me close to you." She then picked up the gold chain with the tiny cross on it and opened the catch.

"Will you put it on for me?" she asked, as she turned her back to Callum.

He put the chain around her neck and fastened it securely.

As Callum and Amy silently made their way home from the airport, Hannah struggled to make sense of the McDonald's till, although her mind kept drifting away from the task in hand. She could think of nothing more than the stupid quarrel between her and Callum and although she regretted making such a crass comment, she felt that his reaction was a little over the top. And she wondered how he and Amy were coping together at the airport. Without her. And she was very angry with herself for even contemplating the thought that perhaps. . .

Michael waited until he could see the lights of Crawley beneath him, before opening the purple envelope and taking out the gold chain which Amy had enclosed. He smiled. Great minds think alike. He put the chain around his neck and fingered it gently. Then he read the love letter which had accompanied it.

Eight

Hannah looked across at the clock on the mantelpiece. It was almost eleven and she was hoping that Callum would call her to say that he and Amy were back from the airport and that Michael was safely on his way to Spain.

She gazed blankly at the TV screen, oblivious to what was on. Her parents had already gone to bed, asking her to keep the volume low as they had an early start the following day. Hannah knew that the phone would disturb them if it rang, but still she willed it to.

There was a strange feeling welling up inside her; the fear that now that Michael had left, things wouldn't be the same between her and Callum. They wouldn't be able to spend so much time together . . . alone. Now that Michael was away, they had to look after Amy. They couldn't just leave her on her own. Wherever they went, whatever they did, they'd have to ask Amy to join them.

And Hannah felt so guilty, that after all these years of friendship, she was now considering Amy to be an intrusion into her new-found relationship with Callum. But she liked Callum . . . *really* liked him. And she felt angry that Michael had had to leave and spoil everything. She stared at the phone again and heard herself saying out loud, "Please ring."

Callum had taken Amy to her door and had left immediately, hurrying to the nearest phonebox. He'd picked up the receiver and was about to call Hannah, but then, realizing what time it was and thinking that her parents might be upset if he rang so late, he'd decided to leave the call until the morning. Anyway, it was possible that Hannah had already gone to bed. She'd be tired after her first evening at work and he didn't want to annoy her by waking her up.

Michael was greeted warmly by his Spanish hosts as soon as he passed through passport control at Madrid's airport. Antonio and Suzana, in their late thirties, were elegantly dressed and Michael felt scruffy and a little uneasy in his T-shirt and jeans as he followed them towards the airport car-park. Antonio walked ahead, pushing the trolley piled high with Michael's luggage, while Suzana spoke to her new house-guest in perfect English.

"I thought Pedro would be with you," said Michael in faltering Spanish. He was tired and the words weren't flowing as he'd hoped they would. But then, it was the first time he'd put his study into practice.

"He's at home, packing his suitcase," replied Suzana, with a smile. "He flies to your home tomorrow lunchtime."

Michael wiped the sweat from his brow. "I hope he's packing plenty of jumpers," he said, returning the smile. "It's been very hot in England, but it probably won't last."

"I know. I've been to London many times on business," she said. "And I've warned him that it's always raining there." She laughed. "We haven't seen any rain here for six weeks."

As they approached the dark blue BMW, Michael checked his watch. It was midnight . . . and it was still so hot. He wondered what the weather would be like at twelve noon in Madrid. Then he realized he hadn't adjusted his watch to Spanish time. It was one o'clock in the morning here.

Antonio began to load the cases into the car's large boot. "You must be tired, Michael," he said. "Don't worry. The drive is only thirty minutes."

Michael tried to reply in Spanish. He couldn't.

Antonio grinned. "English will do," he said. "You can settle in before you start trying the language."

Suzana agreed. "For the first few days we will speak English

84

together, eh? Then we can change to Spanish, when you're ready, Michael."

"And in the middle of the change-over, we can mix it up a little," laughed Antonio. "A little bit of Spanglish!"

Amy had gone to bed as soon as she'd arrived home. But there was no chance of her going straight to sleep. By the light from her bedside lamp, she read his note over and over again. Then she stroked the tiny cross on the gold chain hanging around her neck. She'd been looking forward to the summer holidays so much. A break before she started college. Long, sunny days when she and Hannah could have some real fun, before that worrying transition from schoolgirl to college student. But this was before she'd become involved with Michael. And now she felt totally lost. Michael would be away for the whole of the summer . . . and Hannah had a job. Amy would be alone for five weeks and she wondered how she would fill her days. And she wondered what Michael would be doing at this precise moment. Was he thinking of her, just as she was thinking of him?

She switched off the lamp and lay back, staring up at the ceiling, seeing only his face and that blond hair falling over his bright blue eyes. She could clearly picture his wide smile, and his broad tanned chest, the gold chain she'd given him resting against it. She sighed deeply. Then she closed her eyes and turned on to her side, curling up into a ball, like an infant in its cot. And she cried herself to sleep.

Bypassing the centre of Madrid, Antonio's BMW sped along the motorway to the outskirts of the capital. Michael gazed out of the window, watching the bright lights flashing by, feeling a little disappointed that his stay in Spain wasn't to be in the hub of Madrid. But then he realized that Pedro might also be thinking that he'd be staying close to the Houses of Parliament or Buckingham Palace. Pedro's stay in London would be in the suburbs, just as Michael's stay in Madrid would be in the outskirts.

Looking through his rear-view mirror, Antonio saw the look on Michael's face. "It seems a long way out," he said. "But we have a metro not too far from the house."

"It's probably better not to be in the centre," lied Michael. "I want to see how people in suburbia live."

Suzana laughed. "You mustn't call it suburbia here, Michael," she informed him. "The word 'suburbia' in Spanish means shanty town. And we certainly don't live in an old corrugated-iron hut."

Michael smiled. "Thanks for warning me," he said.

Antonio left the motorway and drove through tree-lined streets to a modern four-storey block of flats, where he parked the car in a underground car-park and leaped out to retrieve the suitcases from the boot.

Pedro was waiting at the lift door as it opened on to the top floor . . . and Michael was immediately struck by how good-looking he was. He looked even better in the flesh than in his photo.

"*Bien venido!* Welcome!" said Pedro as he vigorously shook Michael's hand.

Helping to carry the luggage into the apartment, Pedro babbled away in a mixture of Spanish and English, hardly able to contain his excitement about his visit to London.

"Let me show you my room," said Pedro. "*Your* room, I mean," he added. "It is yours from tonight. I will sleep in another bedroom tonight."

They passed through the huge, modern sitting room, incongruously hung with large paintings of what appeared to be old masters, and along the wide corridor towards the bedrooms.

"How many bedrooms are there?" asked Michael.

"We have six," replied Pedro. "But one of them is used as a changing-room for the maids."

"Maids?" Michael was astounded.

"We have two house assistants," Pedro tried to explain. "But they don't live with us. They arrive at seven o'clock to prepare breakfast and they will be here all day. So if you need anything. . ."

Michael stopped in his tracks and put down the bag he

was carrying. "Pedro," he said, "you do realize that we haven't got anything so grand for you in England, don't you?"

Pedro turned to him and grinned. "No maids?" he laughed.

"No," said Michael, seriously.

Pedro winked at him. "I think I can manage without maids," he said.

They entered the large bedroom and Michael stared incredulously at the furnishings. Framed posters on every wall, an enormous bed – larger than king-sized – a massive flat screen TV, shelves of books, CDs and dvds . . . and an antique writing desk on which was placed the latest computer and printer.

"You also have your own bathroom," Pedro informed him. "*En suite.*"

Michael sighed. "This is incredible!"

"You like it?" beamed Pedro.

"But in comparison to this, I'm afraid you're going to really slum it at my home," said Michael.

"Slummit?" Pedro asked. "What's slummit?"

Michael laughed. "It doesn't matter, Pedro. I'm sure my family will make you feel welcome."

"And now," said Pedro, "let's go and eat some supper. And then you can go to bed."

*

As Michael ate a breakfast of fried eggs served to him by one of the maids, Amy toyed with her piece of toast, wondering what she would do for the rest of the day. Her mother hurried into the kitchen, grabbed her bag and hurried out again. "I'm off," she called. "See you tonight."

Amy was about to reply, when she heard the doorbell ring. She walked into the hall and saw the outline of a man's figure through the glass panelling of the street door.

Mum opened the door and stared at the tall, ginger-haired boy on the step.

"It's OK, Mum," said Amy, from behind her. "It's Callum." She called along the hall. "Come in, Callum."

Mum passed the boy with a smile and hurried out to catch the bus to work.

Callum closed the street door behind him and walked towards the kitchen.

"It's going to be another boiling hot day," he said.

"Great," Amy replied flatly. "Do you want some breakfast?"

"A cup of coffee would be nice," Callum replied.

As Amy reached for the kettle, Callum sat and stared at her. "How are you feeling?" he asked.

She forced a smile. "OK, I suppose."

"Really?"

"No, not really," she replied. "I feel pretty terrible, actually. As soon as I got up, it hit me. He's not here. And I don't know what to do with myself, Callum. It feels so odd without him."

"It must do," said Callum, sympathetically. "I just thought I'd check on you. I knew you'd be a bit down."

"Thanks for looking after me last night," said Amy. "And I'm sorry I burdened you with my bawling."

"No problem." He stood. "Here. I can make that," he said as he reached for the coffee jar.

She handed him a teaspoon. "Have you called Hannah?" she asked.

"No. Not yet. I'll do it before she goes off to work."

"She's working today, is she?" asked Amy, surprised. "I thought she was still training?"

"Doesn't take much training to work a McDonald's till," grinned Callum. "Not for someone like Hannah."

"But she's not working every day, surely?" said Amy. "That's awful. You'll hardly see her."

"That's what *I* said," grimaced Callum. "But she needs the money. She's only doing certain shifts, though," he added. "She's doing the lunchtime one today. So she'll be at home until about half eleven."

"Well, why don't you call her from here?" Amy suggested.

She picked up the phone and dialled.

"Amy! How are you feeling?" asked Hannah. "I was going to call *you*, but I didn't think you'd be up yet."

"I couldn't wait to get out of bed," said Amy. "I was awake

about four and I couldn't get back to sleep again."

"Did he get off all right, last night?" Hannah asked. "Was the flight on time?"

"Yes. No problems."

"So, what time did you get back?" she asked.

"Oh, I don't know," replied Amy. "About eleven, I think."

"I hope Callum saw you home to the door," said Hannah.

"He did. He was so good, Hannah," she replied as she gave a beaming smile across the kitchen to Callum. "I'm afraid I was a bit wimpy. I had a really good cry. But he looked after me."

"I'm glad to hear it," said Hannah.

"Do you want to speak to him?" asked Amy.

The words hit Hannah like a bolt of lightning. "Is he there?"

"Yes."

Hannah tried to force a giggle. It wouldn't come out. "He didn't stay there all night?"

Amy laughed. "Don't be daft. He's just got here. He came to see if I was all right."

"Oh."

"Have a word with him," said Amy as she was about to hand the phone across to Callum.

"No!" said Hannah. She automatically worried that she might have replied too harshly. She softened her voice. "No.

Tell him I'll see him later. He can come over here. Just give me half an hour to get ready."

"Right."

Hannah hung up.

Amy put down the phone. She was surprised and upset by Hannah's comment. Of course Callum hadn't been at the house all night. Surely she didn't think. . .?

"Didn't she want to speak to me?" asked Callum.

"I think she wanted to make herself look pretty for you, Callum," Amy replied. "Give her half an hour."

Callum smiled. "She doesn't need half an hour. She's beautiful enough."

"Aah," giggled Amy. "You really are fond of her, aren't you, Callum?"

"Very," he said, seriously. "I just hope she doesn't let me down."

"Let you down? How do you mean?"

"You know," he said, half stammering. "Dump me for someone else. I don't think I could stand that."

Amy reached out and squeezed his hand. "She won't do that, Callum. She really likes you."

"Do you think so? Honest?"

"Honest."

Callum poured the steaming water from the kettle on to the coffee granules. "So, what are you going to do for the rest of the day?" he asked.

She shrugged. "I've no idea. I'll probably write a letter."

"To Spain?" He laughed. "Already?"

"If it takes a week to get there," she said, "he'll be a whole seven days without hearing from me." She laughed too. "So that's my day taken up. A nice long love letter." She thought. "Don't know what I'll do tonight though."

"We could go to the cinema tonight, if you like," Callum suggested. "Me, you and Hannah."

"You don't want me hanging around with you," she said, softly. "I don't think Hannah'll be very pleased if you tell her that I'm going to come with you on your date."

"Hannah won't mind," said Callum, assuredly.

"Well, how about you ask her first?" said Amy. "If she's happy about the idea, then give me a call this afternoon."

"Will do."

"But if she's not keen, then I want to know. I'm not sitting there, playing gooseberry to you two . . . with Hannah wishing I was a million miles away."

"I'll call you," he said. "But I'm sure it'll be OK."

"No, I don't mind," said Hannah. "Of course I don't mind."

She did mind, but she knew it would be churlish to say otherwise, especially when Amy must be feeling so lonely. "Give her a call, Callum. Tell her I'll go round to her place

93

when I've finished my afternoon stint. About seven. And you can pick us both up from there."

Nine

Michael helped Pedro and his parents carry the luggage to the car. It was strange for Michael to think that in just a few hours Pedro would be sitting in *his* kitchen in England, sipping coffee from *his* mug and chatting with *his* mum and dad. And tonight he would be sleeping in *his* bed. He was concerned that Pedro, used to luxury, would be disappointed by his new surroundings. He was also a little worried that Pedro might take a shine to Amy. No matter what she'd said about the photo, Michael had no doubts that when Amy saw the handsome Spanish boy in the flesh, she would be bowled over.

As the last of the suitcases was packed into the boot, Michael handed Pedro a letter.

"You'll be seeing Amy, Pedro," he said. "My girlfriend. Will you give her this for me?"

Pedro pocketed the sealed envelope. "A love letter, eh?" He smiled. "I make sure she gets it, Michael."

Suzana looked at her watch. "We're late," she said not sounding the least bit hassled.

Pedro shook Michael's hand. "Enjoy your stay," he said. "Everything that's mine is now yours."

"And everything that's *mine* is *yours*," Michael concurred. He paused for thought. "Well . . . almost everything."

Pedro wasn't sure what he meant. "Enjoy España," he said, as he climbed into the car.

Michael watched as Antonio reversed the BMW from its space and manoeuvred it from the underground car park into the street.

Dear Michael, she began.

This is ridiculous, I know, but I'm missing you so much already. I could hardly sleep last night, thinking about you and hoping that you settled in all right. I hope you're not living in some grotty little shack somewhere. It must be really lonely, living with a family of Spaniards and trying to communicate with them. Still, I expect the weather will be nice. It's a beautiful day here. Very hot and sunny again and Callum has already been around this morning to see how I'm

feeling. He suggested that I go to the cinema with him
and Hannah tonight, but I'm not sure about it. I don't
want to get in their way. Anyway, Callum will be ringing
me later to say if it's OK or not. He's going to ask
Hannah. Oh, I do miss you. . .

She stopped writing when she heard the phone ring.

"It's me," said Hannah. "How are you coping?"

"Fine," lied Amy. "I thought you were going to work?"

"I'm off in about five minutes," she replied. "Callum has just left. He was going to call you, but *I* decided to do it instead. Look," she went on, "you mustn't worry about tagging on to us, Amy. You're my best friend. You won't be in the way at all."

"Are you sure? I wouldn't want to. . ."

"Don't be silly, Amy," Hannah tried to convince her. "I'm sure you and Michael would do the same for me if Callum had to go away."

"We would," Amy assured her.

"So, I'll be over to your place about seven and Callum will pick us up from there, OK?"

"In the Mini?" Amy giggled.

Hannah returned the giggle. "I hope not. I've tried to persuade him that we'd be better off on the bus. But who knows?"

"Right. Thanks, Hannah," said Amy, sincerely.

"See you tonight, then."

"See you tonight."

Hannah put down the phone and began to head for the street door. She felt pleased with her good deed. There was no doubt that Amy would be good company. She always was. The two of them had been inseparable for as long as she could remember. And she didn't see why her romance with Callum should break up her greatest friendship.

Having been informed that he'd be left to his own devices for the day, Michael pondered on whether to take the metro into the centre of Madrid or to explore the area in which he was living. Antonio and Suzana had told him that they wouldn't be home until nine o'clock for supper, but as he had his own key, he was to do what ever suited him best. He decided to leave his exploration of Madrid until the following day. It would be better, he felt, to get used to his surroundings in this quiet, villagey kind of suburb. The noonday sun, however, had soon become almost unbearable as he'd strolled around . . . even though he'd worn his baseball cap to keep the rays off his blond head.

Wandering through street after street of modern apartment blocks and detached houses fronted by gardens bedecked with purple bougainvillaea and scarlet hibiscus,

Michael began to get tired. He crossed a sleepy street and passed through a narrow lane where wild geraniums popped up their heads from the large cracks in the walls and pavements. It was a romantic kind of place in which to wander. The perfect spot to stroll arm in arm with someone you really cared for, cut off from the hustle and bustle of the modern world. And he was struck by the irony that Amy would be sitting alone in her house while he wandered, solo, in the ideal setting for two young lovers.

Hannah plunged into despair when she was asked if she would stay on to do the evening session at McDonald's. Although she was grateful for the chance to earn some extra money, she could hardly bear the thought of Callum and Amy spending the evening together . . . without her. She felt strangely jealous that *her* best friend would be out with *her* boyfriend while she had to work. She wondered if she should ring Callum and suggest that the cinema visit be put on hold for another evening. Then she decided to call Amy instead.

"Oh, no," said Amy. "Then let's leave it till you're free, Hannah. I've got plenty of things I can do tonight." Her mind raced. She had *nothing* to do . . . except to finish the already over-long letter to Michael.

"No," replied Hannah, firmly. "You and Callum go. He'll be picking you up just after seven."

"But, I can't!" said Amy. "We can't go without you. It isn't fair."

"What's the point in Callum spending the evening alone?" she asked. "He'll only be getting up to all sorts of mischief. I'd rather you were with him, to keep an eye on him."

"Well, if you're sure?" asked Amy.

"I'll see you at that coffee bar opposite the cinema about ten o'clock," concluded Hannah.

She replaced the receiver and wiped the sweat from her top lip. Her hands were trembling. She'd never felt jealous before. Never. She'd never had any *reason* to feel jealous. Not ever. And she couldn't understand why she was feeling this way now. *Why* was she jealous? Amy wasn't interested in Callum, that was for sure. And Callum wasn't interested in Amy. Was he? *Was* he?

Michael put his linen napkin beside his plate and sat back in his chair feeling satisfied, not only with the amazing meal served by the two rather grumpy maids, but also with his dinner conversation with Antonio and Suzana which had been conducted mainly in Spanish.

"You speak very good Spanish, Michael," Antonio informed him, with a beaming smile. "In five weeks' time, you will be fluent."

"*Gracias*," replied Michael. "I hope so."

"And have you any plans for this evening?" asked Suzana.

Michael looked at his watch. It was ten o'clock. As far as he was concerned, the evening was over, although it was still light outside. "I thought I might watch a bit of television and then go to bed," he said.

Antonio guffawed. "You English! As we Spaniards go out to enjoy ourselves, you English go to sleep."

Suzana agreed. "You're in Spain now, Michael. You must live as the Spanish do. The evening has only just begun."

"Besides," added Antonio, "it's too hot to sleep."

Michael smiled. "You've convinced me. Where can I go?"

"We'll take you to the Torito," suggested Suzana. "It's a bar, a short walk away. Typically Spanish."

"And full of young people," added Antonio. "So we will take you there . . . and you can talk to people of your own age."

"In Spanish, of course," grinned Suzana.

"In Spanish. Definitely!" smiled Michael.

Hannah arrived at the coffee bar and stared across at the foyer, waiting for the film to end and for the cinema-goers to emerge into the warm summer's evening. It was dark now, but the air was clear, the sky filled with stars. A beautiful summer's night. And here she was, waiting, sipping on yet another Coke, sniffing her fingers and hoping that they didn't smell of hamburgers and french fries and Filet-o-Fish. As the cinema suddenly began to turn out its crowd, she scanned the figures under the foyer's bright lights, wondering if she'd see Callum arm in arm with Amy. She watched cuddling couples hurrying down the steps towards their cars, the bus stops and the taxi-rank. And then she saw the familiar heads; ginger and blonde, in intense conversation, a conversation that she wasn't to be part of. And she sighed with relief when she saw that they weren't arm in arm or hand in hand. They began to cross the road towards the coffee bar and when Amy saw her best friend perched on a stool in the window, she smiled, waved frantically and raced across towards her.

Callum immediately wrapped his arm around Hannah's neck and kissed her on the cheek.

"So, how was it?" asked Hannah.

Callum turned up his nose. "Not very good, was it?" he asked Amy.

"Bit slushy," she replied. "All right, I suppose if you're watching it with someone special. . ." She giggled. "Now, if Michael had been with me. . ."

Callum laughed. "But she had to put up with me."

Hannah smiled.

"I'll get some coffees," he said as he headed for the counter.

Amy sat on the stool beside Hannah. "You must be tired," she said.

"I am. But at least I'm not working tomorrow." She sighed. "Thank goodness it's Sunday. I've got the whole day off . . . and the evening too."

"Hey, great!" said Amy. "We should do something." She stopped. "Sorry," she said. "How stupid. You'll want to spend the day with Callum."

She did want to spend the day with Callum. The whole day. And the evening. Just the two of them. "No . . . no, of course I don't," she stammered. "We can all do something together."

"We could go to town for the day," suggested Amy. "I was thinking. Perhaps we should go round to Michael's house and meet Pedro. I promised Michael that I'd call on him. We could take him into London to see the sights. What do you think?"

Hannah beamed. She felt a sudden calm sweep over her. A foursome. She and Callum. Amy and Pedro. It sounded perfect. "Great idea," she said.

The Torito, serving coffee and all kinds of wines and spirits, was full and extremely noisy. Michael had already realized, in his short time in Spain, that they were a very noisy nation. It wasn't so much that the bar's music was being played over-loudly, it was just that the excitable voices of the customers, screeching and shouting across to each other, drowned out any conversation that he and Antonio and Suzana attempted to make. The tiled floor was littered with tiny sugar packets, biscuit wrappings and general rubbish. The custom, it appeared, was simply to discard all these things by dropping them on to the floor, rather than to find a waste bin.

Suzana shrugged when Michael questioned her about it. "It's easier to sweep a floor than to empty bins, don't you think?"

Having left Michael and Suzana sipping on ice-cold orange juices, Antonio crossed the room and spoke to a stocky boy, sweltering in a leather jacket, who was playing the pinball machine. The boy smiled, nodded and finished his game. Then he followed Antonio back to join Michael and Suzana at the bar.

He put out his hand and introduced himself in Spanish. Michael was grateful that, after his short practice with his hosts over dinner, he could understand everything that the boy said to him.

"I'm Santi," he explained. "One of Pedro's friends. How are you enjoying your visit to Spain?"

"I haven't seen much of it yet," Michael replied with a smile.

"So you haven't been into the centre of Madrid yet?"

"No."

"Then we'll go tomorrow," said Santi. "It's Sunday. A good

day for sightseeing." He called across the bar to another boy in his late teens, who approached, drink in hand.

"Juan, this is Michael," he said. "Pedro's exchange partner. What are you doing tomorrow?"

Juan grinned. "Nothing."

"So pass the news around, eh? See how many want to go into the centre for the day. We can all meet at the metro about ten."

"Ten-thirty," Juan corrected him. "It's Sunday. Mass first, eh?"

"For *you*," laughed Santi.

"Si! Mass for me," grinned Juan as he toyed with the small cross hanging around his neck. "Mass and then . . . some fun!" He playfully slapped Michael on the back and then strolled back to join his friends, male and female, on the other side of the bar.

When Antonio and Suzana decided to leave, they persuaded Michael to stay on at the bar.

"It's the best way to learn Spanish," Antonio suggested. He looked at his watch. "And besides, it's still early. You stay here, Michael. Enjoy yourself."

Santi continued to engage Michael in conversation for the rest of the evening, trying at times, unfortunately for Michael, to speak in English. He had great difficulties with the language and Michael found it hard to understand him.

Finally, Santi relented and continued the conversation in Spanish, which was a relief to both of them.

At one o'clock Michael decided to head back to the house. He was feeling very tired and he didn't want a really late night if he was going to spend the next day visiting the centre of Madrid.

"But it's early yet," said Santi. "The bar doesn't close until five o'clock. Anyway, it's Saturday night."

"I'm sure I'll get used to your Spanish ways, Santi," grinned Michael. "But I want my bed!"

Santi laughed and shook his hand. "See you tomorrow," he said. "Ten-thirty. After mass."

As Michael began to leave the bar, he noticed a beautiful girl who was just arriving. In her late teens, she was tall and slim with thick, curly, dark brown hair. On seeing the blond, blue-eyed stranger, she stopped in her tracks and gave him a smile. Flicking back her hair with her fingertips, she stared at him, her dark green eyes twinkling in the lights from the pinball machine.

"Hi!" she said.

"Hi!" he replied.

"Conchita!" a man's voice called from across the bar.

"*Hola!*" Conchita called back. And flashing another quick smile at Michael, she left him at the door and crossed to greet a group of friends.

Michael walked out into the humid, starlit night and, threading his way through the narrow streets, accompanied by the distant sound of a dog baying at the moon . . . and backed by the cicadas gently crooning to each other, he slowly and contentedly made his way home.

Ten

Michael was woken by the high-pitched buzz of a mosquito, hungrily searching the bedroom for some breakfast. Determined that the breakfast wasn't going to be *him,* he leaped out of bed and headed for the shower, glancing at his watch on the way and noting that it was still only six o'clock. Michael had never seen six o'clock on a Sunday morning at home, but then, in England, most mornings were grey, making another two or three hours under the duvet appear so tempting. Even with the unusually hot summer they'd been having back home, six o'clock was never quite as sweaty as this.

Having at last managed to dry off, without even needing to use a towel, he put on his blue shorts and white T-shirt before slipping his trainers on to his sockless feet and heading for the kitchen.

He was surprised to find Antonio and Suzana seated at

the breakfast table, sipping freshly percolated coffee as they flicked through the Sunday newspapers. They looked up at him and smiled.

"Up so soon?" asked Suzana as she rose to fetch another cup for her house-guest. "Or have you only just come in from the Torito?"

Michael laughed. "I'm English!" he said. "Remember? I was in bed by one-thirty."

"You can help yourself to breakfast today," Antonio informed him. "The maids don't work on Sundays. They're good Catholic women and they like to attend mass twice today."

Michael poured some coffee for himself. "Don't you two go to church?" he asked.

"No," replied Antonio. "Pedro used to go, but it wasn't his faith that took him there."

"Oh?" asked Michael. He was curious.

"It was a girl," explained Suzana. "Her family are devout Catholics and she felt that Pedro would be more accepted by her family if he attended the church."

"So does Pedro still have this girlfriend?" asked Michael.

"No. Unfortunately," replied Suzana. "They don't talk any more. And that's a shame, because she was very nice."

Following his hosts' directions, Michael made his way to the old church which stood at the end of the narrow Calle de la Iglesia, its bells tolling and the sun glinting welcomingly off its pale yellow façade. Dozens of people, young and old, were climbing the steep steps to the large portal where they were greeted by the priest, who seemed to know each and every one of them. As Michael passed him, the priest smiled and looked quizzically at him as if to ask, who is this stranger?

"*Hola!*" Michael said to him as he entered the church and took his place in one of the back pews. The church was almost full. The sound of the bells mixed unmusically with both the hymn being hammered out on the organ and the cries of the many young babies. Some of the older women had their heads covered in black shawls and each of the congregation knelt before the altar as they took their seats.

Michael was bowled over by the splendour of the church; its golden altar, the paintings and statuettes and the magnificent stained-glass windows that were bathed in sunlight, making the images seem almost alive. His eyes followed the pews as he searched for Juan, who'd said that he had to attend mass this morning.

He saw him at the front beside the beautiful dark-haired girl who had arrived at the bar last night as he was leaving . . . and he realized immediately that they must be lovers. She sat very close to him, occasionally turning to smile as she touched his arm.

Michael remembered her name. Conchita. Conchita, with the sparkling green eyes, who'd stared at him so strangely. Dressed in black this morning, she looked every inch the story-book Spanish señorita. And as she lifted her black fan to her cheek and flicked it open with such elegance, Michael smiled. This was the Spanish imagery of poetry books; the Spain, which he'd assumed had long since disappeared into the annals of history.

At the end of the service, he left the church confused at the ritual he'd just witnessed. At first he was concerned as to why he couldn't understand what the priest was saying. He could recognize only two or three words in every sentence. Surely his Spanish wasn't *that* bad. Hadn't Suzana and Antonio told him that he spoke very good Spanish? He soon realized that the service was being conducted in Latin.

He found Santi, standing on the steps, grinning wildly.

"So you are a Catholic too!" said Santi.

Michael shook his hand. "Good morning," he said. "No, I'm not a Catholic, Santi. I'm here out of curiosity."

Santi was delighted to be able to use one of the colloquial phrases passed on to him by his English teacher at school. "Curiosity killed the cat!" He guffawed loudly.

"I hope it doesn't kill inquisitive foreigners," replied Michael with a smile.

"I'm waiting for Conchita and Juan," explained Santi. He winked at Michael. "They are both very good Catholics."

"Yes, I saw them in there," replied Michael.

"You know Conchita?" Santi was surprised.

"No," said Michael. "I saw her very briefly last night."

"She's beautiful, no?" asked Santi.

"Very," said Michael.

"I will go to their house with them while Conchita gets changed," he went on. "She won't go into the centre in her black." He laughed. "She looks like a young widow. You can come with us to their home and then we will all go to the metro."

Michael was shocked. "So, Juan and Conchita live together?"

Santi smiled. "Yes. Why not?"

"But if she's a devout Catholic. . . ?" He stopped suddenly, wondering, "They're not married, surely? They're so young."

Santi laughed. "They're brother and sister," he said. "They live with their parents."

Michael suddenly felt relieved. And he wasn't sure why he should feel this way. Why should it bother him? He had no interest in the beautiful girl with the sparkling green eyes. He cared only for Amy. Nobody could hold a candle to her. And he wished that she were here with him now, on the church steps as the congregation emerged, full of grace. His mind wandered. He could almost feel her presence. Amy. Amy and him. Arm in arm. Laughing in the sun and listening to the bells, as they both experienced a typical Spanish Sunday.

Santi grabbed Michael's arm. "I thought he may have told you," he said. "I thought Pedro may have said something."

"Told me what?" asked Michael.

"About him and Conchita," explained Santi. "They were very much in love. They are *still* very much in love."

Michael gasped. "Pedro and Conchita?"

"*Si!* But Conchita says her parents wouldn't approve of him as a future son-in-law. He has no faith, you see. I'm sure that Conchita is wrong. Her parents seem to adore Pedro. But she says they want her to marry a good Catholic boy. And *she* should know."

"But if they love each other?" Michael couldn't understand why they would split up if they really wanted to be together, no matter what Conchita's parents thought.

"Conchita begged him to go back to the church . . . even if it was just a show! But Pedro is stubborn. Like a mule. He wouldn't do as Conchita asked."

"But he has every right," Michael said.

"I agree," said Santi. "Anyway, there was a terrible argument. And Conchita told Pedro that the relationship was over."

113

"Oh. That's sad," said Michael. "And so stupid if you ask me."

Santi shrugged and sighed heavily. "Now both Conchita and Pedro are broken-hearted and I believe it's all for nothing. I'm sure Conchita's parents wouldn't disapprove of Pedro. But obviously, that's what Conchita believes."

Their conversation came to an abrupt end when Juan and Conchita emerged from the church. Conchita was introduced to Michael and as she greeted him with a kiss on the cheek, he smelled her sweet perfume and immediately felt a cold sweat break out on his forehead. This was followed by a deep sense of guilt. He quickly closed his eyes and pictured Amy, wrapped in his arms beside the crackling bonfire in the dark, Kent countryside.

The boys sat in the front garden of Conchita and Juan's old farmhouse where, shaded by the crumbling olive tree, which had long ceased to bear fruit, they waited. Michael hoped to catch sight of the parents, the villains in the romantic tale of Conchita and Pedro . . . the modern-day story of the Montagues and Capulets.

"Are your parents still at mass?" Michael eventually asked Juan.

"They are in Andalucia, visiting relatives," explained Juan. "They are Sevillanos."

Michael looked blank.

Santi explained. "Conchita and Juan's parents were born in Seville. They came north to find work many years ago. And they've remained here for thirty years."

Juan laughed. "Santi is sick of hearing my parents talk of the wonderful times in Seville. They are always promising to return there some day."

"Would you and Conchita ever move south?" asked Michael.

"Never," replied Juan. "Andalucia is truly beautiful. But there is very little work there."

"And Juan and I are Madrileños," said a soft voice from behind them. "We were born in Madrid. This is our home."

Michael looked up to see Conchita, now dressed in scarlet; matching dress and shoes, her hair tumbling beautifully about her shoulders. In her hand she carried a green fan, while a small white bag hung over one arm.

"*Vámanos!*" she said. "Let's go!"

No one else had arrived at the metro by ten-thirty, which didn't surprise Santi. They waited until eleven, as none of their friends, like most Spaniards, were good timekeepers.

"The English are always early," said Juan. "The Germans are always on time. And the Spanish never look at their watches."

At eleven-thirty, they decided to make the journey into

the centre of Madrid alone. Just the four of them: Michael, Santi, Juan . . . and the stunningly beautiful Conchita.

As they approached the Rastro market, all heads turned to stare at the girl in the red dress . . . and the blond-haired, blue-eyed foreigner walking beside her.

The Rastro was packed; the long street was lined with stalls and heaving with wall-to-wall people. It was impossible to move more than a few metres without being held up by the throng. Michael continually removed his shades, wiping the sweat from his stinging eyes and cursing that he hadn't brought his cap to prevent the fierce rays from blistering his scalp. They passed stalls selling all sorts of goods: rugs, furniture, clothes, food, plants . . . and all types of exotic looking birds in cramped wooden cages.

Conchita stopped at a jewellery stall and bartered in rapid Spanish with the stallholder as she held up a pair of crystal earrings. Finally, she threw them down in disgust, obviously believing that the price being asked was far too high. Then, as they began to move off, Michael noticed the tiny gold cross lying on a purple pin-cushion. Realizing that his Spanish wasn't good enough to barter, he asked Conchita to do it for him and, satisfied with the price, he paid the stallholder and pocketed the cross.

Conchita looked at him, enquiringly.

*

Michael's mother was pleased when Amy arrived to ask if Pedro would like to accompany her and her two friends to London for the day. She'd been worried that she'd have to keep the teenage Spaniard occupied when, having been at work all week, she felt that she would have preferred to sit in the garden, reading the Sunday newspapers.

"I'm sure he'll be delighted," she said. "I'll just go and tell him you're here."

Amy strolled down the garden path towards the gate, where Hannah and Callum waited, hand in hand.

"I hope he's all right," said Hannah. "I mean, can he speak English? We're going to have a terrible day if we can't communicate with him, aren't we?"

"Of course he can speak English," replied Amy. "He's been learning it at school. He's over here to improve it, that's all."

The window at the top of the house opened and a voice called out. "Hello. I'm Pedro. *Momento, por favor!*"

Amy looked up, shielding her eyes from the bright sunlight, trying to get a good look at the boy whose photo she'd already seen. He disappeared from view and closed the window.

Hannah gasped, looked at Amy and giggled. "Did you see him?" she asked.

"No. Not really," replied Amy.

"*I* did," said Callum, huffily.

"What's the matter, Callum?" asked Amy.

"Nothing," he replied, flatly.

Hannah shrieked with laughter. "I think Callum's a bit jealous," she said. She mock-whispered to Amy, "Our Pedro looks a bit tasty."

"Don't be stupid!" snapped Callum. "I'm not in the slightest bit jealous."

"And it wouldn't matter to me how 'tasty' Pedro is," smiled Amy. "We're just being nice to him for Michael's sake." She wagged a finger at Hannah, as a joke warning. "So just you remember that, Hannah."

"*Moi?*" giggled Hannah. "*I'm* not interested in him. Why should I be?" She cuddled up to Callum. "Not when I've got my hunky redhead. It's *you* I'm worried about, Amy. After all, it's *you* who's going to be alone for five weeks."

"*Hola!*" yelled Pedro as he hurried down the path towards them, dressed in red shorts and a white T-shirt.

Amy stared, open-mouthed at the gorgeous face, the dark brown eyes below the short, jet-black hair, the dazzling white smile . . . and the strong, tanned legs.

"Hi!" she gulped. "So you're Pedro!"

Eleven

On the train to Charing Cross, the four chatted constantly, and when they'd arrived, it felt, strangely, as though Pedro had always been part of their lives. He was extremely easy to talk to and had a sense of humour which appealed to them all, particularly to Callum. Amy was keen to know about Pedro's home life, knowing that this would enable her to picture Michael more easily, in his new environment.

"Hey! I almost forgot," said Pedro as he rummaged in the shoulder-bag he was carrying. "Michael sent this to you." He handed the sealed envelope to Amy, whose heart suddenly began to pound, rapidly.

"A love letter!" shrieked Hannah. "What's it say?"

Callum took Hannah's hand and squeezed it affectionately. "I think Amy may want to keep that to herself, don't you?"

"I'll look at it later," said Amy, who was bursting to open it.

She tucked it into the back pocket of her jeans, hoping that there would be a quiet moment in the day when she would be able to read it in private.

Heading along the Strand, they reached Covent Garden, which was bustling with tourists, some Americans but mainly Europeans . . . and here they decided to take coffee at one of the pavement cafés.

Pedro, struck by Amy's beauty, made a concerted effort to take in all three of his companions as he talked to them, aware that, at first, Amy had received too much attention from him. He'd even found himself, at one stage, on the edge of flirting with her, although he was sure that she hadn't realized what he was doing. He stopped immediately. He didn't want to offend her . . . nor her friends.

Besides, from the way that Amy had talked about Michael on their journey to town, it was obvious that she was very much in love with him. Any advances from Pedro, no matter how slight, would be spurned. That was for sure.

He remembered that this was how he used to behave before he met Conchita: flirting with any pretty girl he came across. She'd changed all that. As soon as their relationship had begun, he hadn't looked at anyone else. What was the point? Conchita was everything he wanted. She was beautiful, strong-willed and fun to be with. And he'd felt sure that they'd always be together. To dump him, unceremoniously, as she did, had come as a terrible shock.

He still couldn't believe it had happened. When she'd said it was all over, it was like a dagger to his heart. And when the offer of the exchange visit to London was offered, he'd leaped at the chance, hoping that by distancing himself from her and all their mutual friends, it might give him the time he needed for the wounds to heal. Now he was a free agent. He could, if he wished, return to his old ways. And if only Amy wasn't so in love with Michael, then. . .

As the waiter brought their coffee, Amy asked him where the ladies were.

"I won't be a minute," she said to the others. Then, as soon as she was in private, she opened Michael's letter and began to read:

Dear Amy,

I'm missing you already. I just thought I'd let you know that I'm not living in a shack. The house is beautiful and is on the outskirts of Madrid. I have my own room with an en suite *shower and, would you believe it, I have maids to cook and clean up after me. It's incredible the way some people live, isn't it? I think I'm going to be happy here.* Fairly *happy. My happiness could only be complete if you were here with me. I just keep thinking of all the things we could do together, if only you could have come to Spain too. It just seems ridiculous for you*

*to spend your summer there, alone in London, especially
as your parents will be going away to France. And here,
there are so many bedrooms. What do you think? Is there
any chance that you could come over? Pedro's parents,
Antonio and Suzana, are so nice. I'm sure they'd be
happy about having another house-guest. Anyway,
please think about it. Seriously. It would be great if you
were with me. Pedro seems very nice, I must say. By the
time you read this, you will, of course, have met him.
Pretty hunky, isn't he? I hope you don't fall for him. I'm
sure he'll go mad when he sees you. But then, who
wouldn't? I miss you and love you and can't wait till
we're back together again.*

    All my love, for ever, Michael

Amy sighed, put the letter back into its envelope and slipped
it into her pocket. Her mind was racing. Was there a chance of
going to Spain? She had some savings in her post office
account. So that was no problem. But she was pretty sure her
parents wouldn't approve. They liked Michael, but there was
no way they'd let her go to Spain to join him. Still, there was
no harm in asking. She'd do it tonight.

"Your coffee's cold," said Callum as Amy returned, looking
slightly flushed.

"I expect you've been reading Lover Boy's letter, haven't

you?" asked Hannah, twinkling. "So, what's it say?"

"Hannah!" Callum reprimanded her.

Amy smiled and sipped on the cold coffee, saying nothing.

Sunday in Madrid's beautiful Retiro Park was the most popular day for the strolling Madrileños. Juan grabbed a table at the cafe facing the great lake and all four sat under the shade of a parasol, ordering a lunch of cold drinks and *tapas*.

Michael took out the tiny gold cross from his pocket and put it on the table. Then, releasing the catch from Amy's gold chain around his neck, he removed it and carefully slipped the cross on to it.

Conchita watched him, wide-eyed. "Are you a Catholic?" she asked.

Michael was surprised at her question. "No. Why?"

"Oh." She sounded disappointed. "I saw you at Mass. And I thought that the gold cross. . ."

Michael began to put the chain around his neck "No. This is for someone special," he explained "And I only went to Mass because I was curious."

"But you *believe*," she said. "You have faith. You must believe, or you wouldn't wear a cross."

"I'm not sure what I believe," replied Michael almost dismissively. "I'm wearing this chain simply because it was given to me by someone I love very much."

The waiter arrived with a tray of drinks and half a dozen small white dishes which he put on the table.

"What are these?" Michael asked, as he stared, with some trepidation, at the dishes.

"A mixture of all sorts," grinned Santi, aware that most Englishmen would rather tuck into burgers and fries than anchovies or garlic-soaked olives.

Michael picked up the tiny fork and dug into the anchovy dish, dropping a few of them into his mouth and grimacing at the taste.

"They're so salty," he said as he quickly washed them down with a mouthful of Coke.

Conchita laughed and took a forkful of peas and chopped ham. "This will be better for your delicate English tongue," she said as she leaned forwards and placed the fork at Michael's lips. He took them into his mouth . . . and chewed.

"Better?" she asked.

"Much," he grinned.

There was the sound of a tambourine and looking up they saw a young girl, hand in hand with a clownish figure dressed in white.

"It's a pierrot," Conchita shrieked excitedly.

The young girl took a step back as the clown began, in silence, to perform his magic tricks. He produced silk scarves

124

and cards and eventually a small white dove from his sleeve, to the approval of the crowd now gathering around the café. Then reaching inside his white jacket, the pierrot placed his hand on his heart and peeled off a small red balloon which he began to inflate by the use of a tiny pump. The balloon slowly expanded until it resembled a large red love-heart.

"Aaah!" said the crowd as one, before laughing and then applauding loudly.

The pierrot tied a piece of string on to the heart-shaped balloon and then handed it to the smiling Conchita before moving off to find another audience on the other side of the park. His young female companion lingered for a while, holding out her tambourine and gratefully receiving the few coins that some of the audience placed there.

Conchita looked wistfully at the balloon.

"Why do I think you're thinking of Pedro?" asked Juan.

Conchita immediately let go of the balloon, and the four of them watched it as it sailed into the air and across the lake.

"Perhaps your heart will fly all the way to London," Juan said softly.

"Perhaps," Conchita replied.

From Covent Garden, Pedro was led to Trafalgar Square by his English guides, on towards Buckingham Palace and then back to Green Park where they strolled along the water's edge, watching the ducks and moorhens frolicking in the sun. As they crossed the tiny bridge, Hannah spied a discarded lolly-stick and screeching with delight, she picked it up and dropped it over the side, watching the water below carry it under the bridge and out of view. She and Callum then peered over the other side of the bridge and waited, like two young children, for their stick to reappear on top of the fast-flowing water.

"There it is!" screamed Hannah.

Amy looked at Pedro and tutted. "They're like two kids."

Pedro questioned her, "Kids? Baby goats?"

Amy laughed. "Yes. Baby goats."

As Hannah and Callum busied themselves looking for more debris to throw over the bridge, Amy took the opportunity to inform Pedro of Michael's suggestion.

"I think it's a very good idea," replied Pedro. He gazed into her eyes, seeing only Conchita's eyes looking back at him. Secretly he hoped that she wouldn't go to Spain. It was exciting being in the company of someone as beautiful as Amy. Exciting, but dangerous. "I'm absolutely sure that my parents wouldn't mind," he added. "We have plenty of room and they're both very free-thinking people. I think they would welcome you with open arms."

Amy began to tremble with excitement. Was it possible? Could she spend the summer with Michael in Madrid?

"Hey!" yelped Callum suddenly. "Who wants an ice-cream?"

Hannah had also spotted the ice-cream stall set up outside the park gates. "Me, please!" she said.

"I'll come with you, Callum," said Pedro. "The two girls can stay here and throw sticks into the water like . . . baby goats."

As they watched Callum and Pedro amble towards the gates, Hannah whispered, as though it were some great secret. "He really is hunky, isn't he?"

Amy laughed. "I assume you mean your Callum?"

"Oh, he's lovely, is Callum," replied Hannah. "I wouldn't swap him for the world. But no, I wasn't talking about Callum, Amy."

"Yes, he's very gorgeous," agreed Amy. "When Michael showed me the photo I knew that he was quite good-looking, but. . ."

"And he's certainly taken a fancy to you," chortled Hannah.

"Don't be daft," laughed Amy. "What makes you say that?"

"He can't take his eyes off you," said Hannah. "Every time I look at him, he's staring at you."

"Nonsense!" she said. "You're making it up."

"You'll see," grinned Hannah. "I bet he makes a move on you. Just give him a few days."

Amy glared at Hannah. "I don't want him to make a move on me, as you so delicately put it, Hannah. I'm not in the slightest bit interested in him. Anyway, I may not be here for much longer."

Hannah was shocked. "What do you mean?"

"That letter. From Michael."

"Yes?"

"He's asked me to go out to join him in Spain."

"No!" Hannah gasped. "And?"

"I'd love to, but I'll have to ask my mum and dad."

Hannah shook her head, sadly. "They'll never let you. You know how protective your parents are. They won't let you go off abroad on your own."

"Well, I'm going to try," said Amy. She looked up at Hannah, with tears in her eyes. "I don't think I can stand five weeks without him. I'm going to ask my mum and dad tonight."

"Well, I'll keep my fingers crossed for you," said Hannah. "But don't raise your hopes."

Amy waited until her father had left for his nightly visit to the pub, before broaching the subject.

"I had a letter from Michael today," she said to her mother. Her mouth was dry. She sipped on her coffee and continued. "His exchange partner, Pedro, brought it over for me."

Amy's mother pointed the remote control at the TV screen and changed channels, only half-listening to her daughter.

"That was nice of him," she said.

"Anyway, he's living in this really big place. . ."

"Don't want this, do we?" Mum asked, referring to the TV programme.

"Erm . . . I don't mind," replied Amy.

Mum pressed the remote again.

"So, I wanted to tell you something, while Dad was out. Well, *ask* you something, really."

Mum suddenly began to pay attention. She was worried about what she was going to hear. She turned the sound off the TV and put down the remote. "What?"

"It's just that. . ."

"There's nothing wrong, is there?" Mum was concerned.

"No. There's nothing wrong."

"But this is to do with you and Michael?"

"Yes."

Amy's mother's eyes widened. She began to pale slightly. "You're not. . . ?"

Amy was annoyed. "No! I'm not. Don't be ridiculous. I'm not stupid, Mum!"

Mum guiltily looked back at the silent screen. "Sorry. I just thought for a minute. . ."

"Michael has asked if I'll go to Spain," Amy blurted out. "There's plenty of room in the house and. . ."

"No!" her mother replied, firmly. "Definitely not."

"But why?" It was the answer that she'd expected, but she was hoping to talk her mother round.

"You can't come to France with us," snapped her mother, "but you can go off to Spain to spend time with a boy you've known for five minutes!"

"Mum!" pleaded Amy. "Think about it. Please. It'll be a great experience for me . . . and once I start college I may not get another chance like this."

"No!" said her mother. "And it's no good trying to soft-soap me while your father's out, because we'd both agree about this one. You're not going. And I don't want to hear any more about it."

Amy silently left the room.

TWelve

During the ten days that he'd been in Madrid, Michael had spent most of his time in the company of Conchita, although Juan was always nearby, acting as a chaperone to his younger sister. Both were on holiday from college, free to show Michael the areas around Madrid which he'd never have seen without them. Santi joined them most evenings, but during the day he had to work – a school holiday job in the local bakery, which he continuously complained about.

Michael had seen and learned the history of Toledo, Escorial and The Valley Of The Fallen and with help from his new friends, he'd found that his Spanish had really improved. Even Antonio and Suzana had dropped their 'Spanglish' and were now only speaking to him in Spanish. They hoped that Pedro, who seemed to be enjoying his stay in London, was working as hard as Michael at improving his language skills.

Amy's letter had bitterly disappointed Michael. He'd been

so excited about everything he'd seen and done and although he'd try to share his excitement in the letters he regularly sent to her, he longed for her to be by his side, tasting the delights of Spain with him. He thought about her constantly, even though there were times, when in deep conversation with Conchita, he'd felt he wanted to reach out and take the beautiful Spanish girl in his arms. These desires were immediately followed by feelings of profound guilt. He loved Amy so much and he knew he could never do anything to hurt her. But Conchita's dark green eyes, staring into his, as she chatted and smiled and playfully stroked his arm, were almost . . . hypnotic.

On his one day off Santi had borrowed his father's car and had offered to take his three friends on an adventure drive. They met at El Torito in time for morning coffee and set off around eleven o'clock, leaving Madrid and driving through the tunnel towards Segovia. As Juan had decided to ride in the front passenger seat, Michael sat in the back beside Conchita, who today was dressed in khaki shorts and a pale green T-shirt. She wore no make-up and her pale olive face shone as the morning heat grew in intensity. Michael felt the sweat running down the back of his legs and was grateful that he'd decided to wear his shorts rather than his jeans.

As they approached the huge Roman aqueduct at the

entrance into the city, Michael felt Conchita's leg brushing against his. At first he was sure that it was Santi's erratic stop-start driving which had simply forced Conchita to change position in the bumpy back seat. He waited for her to move her leg. She didn't. He was sure that she was pressing it closer to his. He began to sweat even more, wondering if he should move away from her, fearful that Juan, gazing through the windscreen at the magnificent aqueduct, would become aware of his laboured breathing. He tentatively reached across and placed his hand on top of Conchita's, waiting for her to brush it aside with a giggle.

There was a deathly silence for minutes, both of them now peering out of their respective windows, admiring the scenery. Finally, he felt her gently squeeze his hand. He responded by doing the same, as he turned to look at her. She gave no reaction. He wondered what was going on in her mind. And he worried that behind her dark shades, those hypnotic green eyes were laughing at him.

"Beautiful, isn't she?" said Juan, quite suddenly.

Michael immediately withdrew his hand.

"The aqueduct," added Juan. "Beautiful, isn't she? A stunning piece of architecture."

"She's *extremely* beautiful," replied Michael. He looked at Conchita, sure that she'd respond with a smile. She didn't move. Staring straight ahead she sighed deeply . . . and

Michael watched as a tear ran from under her shades and down her cheek.

Hannah was extremely disappointed that on the day they'd all chosen to travel to the Sussex coast, the flu-bug had caused a staff shortage at McDonald's and the manager had asked her to work. She rang Callum's home and suggested they all went without her.

"I don't want to go without you," said Callum, plaintively. "Can't you refuse? Can't you say that you've got flu too?"

"I can't, Callum," she replied. "They're in such a state here."

"But *I've* got to go, Hannah; you do realize that, don't you? They'll be so disappointed if I cancel now."

"I know," she said. "Of course you've got to go with them. But as you're walking along Brighton beach, just you think about me saying, 'Enjoy your meal,' for the thousandth time."

Callum laughed. "I'll miss you," he said.

"Yes. Just make sure that you do," she replied with a chuckle. "I'll see you tomorrow."

Passing through the narrow, higgledy-piggledy streets of Segovia, they finally took their seats at a pavement café and gazed up at the distant Alcazar, with its conical towers making it appear like some sort of Disneyland castle.

"I'm half expecting Mickey Mouse to come skipping along

the road and grab my hand," said Michael.

"It's a bit older than Disneyland, Michael," grinned Santi. "And its stories aren't so cosy. It's perched on the side of a deep precipice and in the fourteenth century a nanny accidentally dropped a baby she was looking after, over the edge."

"How clumsy of her," grinned Michael.

His Spanish companions didn't laugh.

"She was so distressed," continued Santi, "that she threw herself over the edge too. No, it certainly isn't Disneyland," he added.

Michael couldn't take his eyes from the structure. It was the picture he'd seen in every childhood story-book. The castle where the Prince finally took Snow White to live happily ever after. The home of Cinderella's Prince Charming. The castle where Sleeping Beauty lay asleep for a hundred years until her prince woke her with a kiss.

"It's an amazing building," said Juan, as he grabbed the camera from his bag. "I'm going to take some photos. Coming?"

"Later," replied Conchita. "I want to finish my coffee."

Santi followed Juan. "We'll meet you at the top of the hill when you're ready," he called back.

Michael nodded at them with a smile, but didn't attempt to move. He had to be alone with Conchita for a few minutes.

He had to find out what had been going through her mind when she'd gently squeezed his hand.

Left alone with him, she was obviously embarrassed.

He tried to make light of the situation, joking, "You'd look good in that fairy-tale castle. The Sleeping Beauty's got nothing on you."

She didn't reply.

"Being woken up by some handsome prince. . ."

She sighed.

"What's wrong, Conchita?" he asked her, softly.

She refused to look at him, staring ahead at the passers-by. "Nothing's wrong."

"Please," he said. "Talk to me. Tell me why you did that. Tell me what's making you so unhappy."

She slowly removed her sunglasses and turned to face him. Her eyes were cloudy. "Oh, Michael," she tried to explain, speaking in English. "I'm very sorry. I think you may have misunderstood me. I should never have held your hand like that. I don't want you to think. . ." She stopped and looked away again.

"Think what?" he replied, also in English. "That you were coming on to me?"

She smiled. "Coming on to me? What does that mean?"

He smiled too. "I don't know how to say it in Spanish. So perhaps it's better if I don't try to translate it, eh?"

"I miss Pedro so much," she said, suddenly. "I love him,

Michael. And I'm so very, very lonely without him."

Michael was stunned into silence.

"Every day I miss him. And I wish I could go back a few months . . . when everything was all right."

"But a few months back or a few years forward, the problem will still be there, Conchita," he said. "Your parents can't force him into a religion he doesn't believe in."

"I know," she said. "The problem will always remain, Michael."

He shook his head in despair. "I really don't understand," he said.

She stood, her sunglasses dangling delicately from one hand and began to walk away from him. "No. I don't suppose you do," she replied.

He followed her. "Conchita!"

She stopped. "We'd better go and join the others," she said.

He firmly gripped both her arms in his hands and stared into her eyes. "Conchita," he said softly.

"Michael," she replied, "don't. Please."

He kissed her . . . and he felt no response. He stepped back and looked at her, deeply ashamed. "Sorry," he said. "I'm very sorry."

She lowered her voice to a whisper. "You love Amy. And in spite of everything, I still love Pedro. I always will."

"Yes, I know," he said. "I'm sorry."

"So, let's forget this happened, eh?" she suggested. "And now, we really must go and find Santi and Juan."

Callum wandered along the promenade behind Amy and Pedro, wishing that Hannah was with them. At times he stopped to watch the children splashing about in the sea or filling up their buckets with pebbles. And whenever he stopped, he was aware that Pedro and Amy simply strolled on without him. For most of the time they were oblivious to his presence. And this began to worry him. He was suddenly aware that the two of them appeared to be getting very . . . close. He hoped they weren't becoming *too* close. He began to panic. Surely Amy hadn't fallen for Pedro? No. She couldn't! That would break Michael's heart.

When they left the promenade and sat on the shingled beach, gazing out at the clear horizon, Callum sat beside them, saying nothing. He wasn't sure if he should, when he had the chance, let Amy know of his fears. But then he decided that he'd leave that to Hannah. After all, she was Amy's best friend, and if something had to be said, it would be better coming from her.

He looked at his watch, wondering if it was time they all went and found somewhere to have lunch. Then he remembered. The car. He had to return to the parking meter to put in some more money. He cursed. This day out was

138

costing him a fortune. And while he wouldn't have bothered about the expense if he and Hannah were enjoying a day at the coast together, today he felt as though he were being used. He'd been nothing more than a chauffeur. They didn't even seem to want his company now that they'd arrived at their destination.

"I'll be back in a while," he said. "I've just got to go and feed the meter."

"Hang on," replied Amy as she searched in her bag for her purse. "I'll give you some money. I don't see why you should pay for everything, Callum."

"And I will pay for the petrol," added Pedro, "and buy us all some lunch."

"Thanks," said Callum as he took Amy's money with a smile and left, feeling guilty. "I won't be long."

As he hurried off, Pedro stared after him. "He's a nice guy," he said. "I don't think *I'd* have come all the way to Brighton, if my girlfriend couldn't come with me."

"Aah, but you don't have a girlfriend," said Amy, dismissively.

Pedro fell strangely silent.

Amy stared at him. "What's up?" she asked. Then it hit her. She suddenly realized. For the first time in the ten days she'd known him, she was aware that he had someone back home. Someone he cared for. "You *do*, don't you?" she said. "You do have a girlfriend?"

"No," he replied. "I don't. There is someone who I love very much, but. . ."

Amy sounded sympathetic. "But she doesn't love you." It was a statement, not a question.

"She *does* love me," argued Pedro. "We both love each other."

"But why haven't you told me?" asked Amy. She immediately felt stupid at asking such a ridiculous question. Why *should* he have told her? It had nothing to do with her.

"Because it has ended," he said. "We love each other, but we cannot be together."

"But why?" asked Amy.

"It is too difficult," he said. He looked at her, sadly. "I don't want to talk about it today. Today it is too nice a day to talk about it. We should enjoy the sunshine and the beach . . . and each other's company. Someday I will tell you."

"But she *is* Spanish?" asked Amy.

He sighed. "Yes. Her name is Conchita and she is very, very beautiful. She lives in Madrid, very near to my house."

"Really?" Amy was surprised. "So Michael's probably met her?"

"Michael *would* have met her, yes," replied Pedro. "Without doubt. Conchita and I have many mutual friends. And I'm sure Michael will have met some of them. And therefore he will have met Conchita."

"And he'll know that you and Conchita were lovers?"

"Yes. I'm sure he'll know," said Pedro. "It's not a secret."

Amy gazed into space. Her mind was racing. This was all very strange. If Michael had met Pedro's girlfriend, why hadn't he mentioned it in his letters?

Unless. . .?

Thirteen

The sun was just beginning to set as Santi drove his companions back towards Madrid. Michael stared in awe through the back window at the blood-red sky and for a brief moment he blocked out the hurt he'd felt when Conchita had insisted on sitting in the front. He'd hoped that they'd both be able to forget the snatched kiss; that they could still be friends. But now he wondered if she'd decided to turn her back on him . . . literally; that they would no longer be spending any time together.

He shivered. Then recovered. Perhaps it was for the best. He still loved Amy . . . so, so deeply . . . and although this beautiful girl had, for a while, captivated him, he now knew for certain where his heart lay. He wished that Amy were with him, gazing out at the sunset, watching the swallows darting to and fro and the large, red kites circling overhead searching for supper. He wanted to share with her this feeling of intoxication, brought about by the incredible sights and sounds and smells.

Juan gently dug him with his elbow. "It's beautiful, eh?"

"Beautiful," agreed Michael.

"But you've seen nothing yet," added Juan. "You haven't seen the *real* Spain."

Santi looked through his rear-view mirror and sneered jokingly at Juan "*Qué va!*" he said. "What nonsense! This is *all* the real Spain."

Juan laughed. "Santi gets angry when I talk of the *real* Spain, Michael," he explained. "He knows I'm talking about Southern Spain; Andalucia."

"And as I come from Barcelona in the north," continued Santi, "I find this a great insult."

Conchita turned her head to look at Michael, smiling at him for the first time since they'd left Segovia. "Juan is right," she said. "You must see Andalucia while you're here."

"You must visit Seville," Juan went on. "I would never leave Madrid, for sure. That is my home and I love it there. But to visit Seville, the homeland of my parents and my grandparents, is a must for any visitor to Spain."

Santi tutted. "Flamenco and gypsies and bullrings."

"We could take him there, Juan," Conchita suggested enthusiastically. She addressed Michael. "We could stay with

143

our grandparents for a few days. Would you like that, Michael? You could meet our parents at the same time."

"I'd love it," Michael replied. "But if your parents are already staying there, will there be enough room? Won't your grandparents mind?"

"There's plenty of room," said Conchita. "And my grandparents will be very happy to meet you." She turned to Santi and teasingly placed her hand on his knee. "I'm sure Santi could borrow his father's car for a few days."

Santi shook his head. "I'm sure he *can't*," he grinned.

"Then we'll take a bus," smiled Conchita. "*No hay problema.*"

On their return from Brighton, Callum, although feeling very tired, offered to drive Amy and Pedro to their respective homes.

"I'm sure you want to go straight off to see Hannah," said Pedro. "You can drop us both at Amy's house. I can walk from there."

"No, it's no problem," Callum said quickly while trying to stifle a yawn. "I'll take you home, Pedro."

"Don't be silly, Callum," said Amy. "You've done enough driving for one day. I'm sure Pedro won't mind walking home from my place."

Callum began to worry about leaving them alone together.

He could think only of the promise he'd made to Michael . . . to look after Amy. And he wasn't fulfilling that promise!

"I insist," said Pedro. "I shall enjoy the walk, Callum."

Reluctantly leaving them at Amy's path, Callum turned the car around and headed for Hannah's house. He'd decided not to tell Hannah how concerned he was about Amy and Pedro. Not tonight. Hannah would probably suggest that they went back to Amy's house on some pretext, just to make sure that Pedro had gone straight home. Callum sighed. He wanted to protect Michael's interests, but not if it meant interfering with his own relationship with Hannah. He'd spent all day with Amy and Pedro. He'd done all he could. And now it was *his* time. He wanted to be alone with Hannah, to hold her in his arms, to ask about her day, to tell her once again that he loved her. He'd certainly tell Hannah his worries. But it would have to wait until tomorrow. He didn't want to think about Amy and Pedro for the next hour or so. He didn't even want to think about Michael.

"Would you like to come in for some coffee?" Amy asked him.

Pedro looked at his watch. "No. I think I'd better get home. Can I see you tomorrow?" he asked.

"Of course," she replied. "I don't know what plans Hannah and Callum have, but I'm sure we can sort out something exciting to do."

"It's been a very enjoyable day," he said. "I really like your company, Amy. And Callum's too," he added quickly, sounding a little embarrassed.

"And *I* like *your* company, Pedro," Amy said with a smile. Her heart skipped a beat. She stared into his dark eyes . . . and immediately began to panic. Oh Michael, why aren't you with me, she thought. I don't like what's going on here.

Pedro stepped forward and put his arms around her. "Are you all right?" he asked. "You seem a little sad."

She closed her eyes and pictured Michael wrapping his arms round her, pulling her closer towards him. She could feel his broad chest pressing against hers. She could see his gorgeous tanned face below the mop of blond hair . . . and the bright, blue eyes, clouding slightly as he leaned forward to kiss her. She saw him smile and she heard his voice whisper, "I love you, Amy."

"I'm fine, Pedro," she croaked. "Honestly, I'm fine."

"Well, goodnight," he said softly. He kissed her lightly on the cheek. Then he turned and walked away.

Amy sat at the kitchen table, writing her daily letter to Michael. She could hear her parents crashing around upstairs, packing their cases for their holiday in France. She wished now that she'd planned to go with them, despite her reservations about camping. At least it would have meant saying goodbye to Pedro . . . before things got out of control! What was the point now, she wondered, in hanging around here without Michael by her side? When she'd originally refused the offer, she'd thought that she and Hannah would be having a great time together. But that was before they'd both fallen in love.

Dear Michael,

I've just got back from Brighton and I've had a great day, although naturally it would've been so much better if you'd been there. I really miss you. More than you can imagine. My parents are off to France tomorrow and in a way I wish I was going with them now. Knowing you'd be just down the road in Spain would've made the campsite a little more bearable. Still, it's too late now. Hannah and Callum are being great to me, although Hannah spends too much time working, leaving poor Callum with time on his hands.

Pedro seemed to enjoy Brighton, although I think he found it strange sitting on pebbles rather than those sandy beaches they have in Spain. He's really nice, Michael. I like him a lot. I don't want you to get the wrong idea, but I'm very pleased that you and I are going out together, because if not, I might have got to really like him . . . if you know what I mean. And that would've been a disaster, because of course, he'd have to go back to Spain eventually and that would've been very upsetting. . .

Oh, dear . . . I've just read this letter back and it looks as though I've fallen for Pedro, which I haven't. I was in two minds whether or not to tear it up and start again, but then I thought that that would be dishonest in a way. I'm only telling you my feelings because if we have a future together, we have to be honest with each other and say exactly how we feel. I do find him quite attractive, I must say. You knew I would. But of course, if you were here, I wouldn't have even given him a second glance. Oh, I do love you, Michael. And I wish the days would speed by so that we're back together again. Pedro was telling me all about his ex-girlfriend called Conchita. He said that you would've met her out there. I'm just surprised that you haven't mentioned her in your letters. I hope it's not because you've fallen for her (ha ha . . . as if you would). Anyway, I'll close now and get this into the post first thing in the morning.

All my love,
Amy

She put the letter in an envelope, stuck on a stamp and, on the way up to bed, she left it on the hall table beside several other letters waiting to be posted. Her father passed her on the staircase.

"Finished packing?" she asked.

He sighed. "Nearly. Mum said she'd do the rest. I'm gasping for a pint."

"You're not going to the pub at this time of night, are you?" she asked, surprised.

He looked at his watch. "It's only ten o'clock," he grinned. "Plenty of time before last orders."

She passed her parents' bedroom and eyed her mother trying to squeeze a huge bath towel into an already bulging suitcase.

"Night, Mum," she said and she went into her room and sat on the edge of her bed, thinking. She hoped Michael wouldn't be upset when he read her latest letter. Perhaps it'd been a bit stupid to be quite so honest. If Michael felt that she was two-timing him . . . he'd be distraught. It might ruin the fun he was having in Spain. He might even feel that if *she* had her eye on someone else, then he would do the same. She suddenly felt her breathing becoming shallow. She took a huge gasp of air, trying to control it. Her hands began to tremble. Why hadn't he mentioned Conchita? Surely he wasn't. . . ? No. Not Michael.

She lay back on her bed and thought about the wonderful

days they'd spent together, particularly the day at Bluebell Wood; sitting beside the fire they'd built as they waited for Callum's dad to arrive. She closed her eyes and slept.

She woke with a start, wondering where she was. The light was on and she was still fully clothed. She looked at her watch. It was only eleven-fifteen. She sat up. And she remembered. The letter. What a ridiculous thing to do. She couldn't possibly send a letter like that. What was she thinking? How stupid! She hurried from her room and down the stairs to the hall table. The letter wasn't there. Perhaps her mother had moved it for some reason. She felt slightly uneasy as she approached the kitchen where she found her mother making a bedtime drink.

"I thought you were asleep," her mother said.

"I was reading," Amy lied. "Dad not back yet?" she asked.

"He's probably got talking to his mates down the pub," she smiled. "Anything to get out of packing. You know how much he hates it."

"You haven't seen my letter around, have you?" asked Amy, a slight tremor in her voice.

"What letter?"

"I left it on the hall table with all those others."

Mum looked up. "I asked your dad to post them on the way to the pub," she said. "He must've posted yours as well."

Amy paled.

Dear Amy, he wrote.

*I'm very excited. We've had a great day today. Some
good Spanish friends took me to Segovia which was
fantastic. Anyway, they've now suggested we all go off to
Seville together. I can't wait. I've always wanted to see
Andalucia . . . and particularly Seville. We're going by
bus, so it should be an interesting journey. By the time
you read this, I'll be there, watching all those flamenco
dancers and maybe even visiting. . .*

Fourteen

Amy received Michael's letter a week later and she immediately began to panic. She'd had many sleepless nights about the letter *she'd* sent *him*, and now, knowing that it was probably sitting in Madrid waiting for his return from Seville, she felt even worse. He hadn't even seen it yet. And when he'd read it, how would he feel? She hadn't written a word to him since that night. She didn't know where to start. She'd spent most of her days and some evenings with Pedro, but always in the company of either Hannah or Callum . . . or both. She didn't want to be alone with Pedro. She missed Michael so much. She ached to see him again. But she also felt that if Pedro suddenly made any sort of romantic advance towards her, then. . .

Surprised that the phone was ringing so early in the morning, Amy rushed to answer it, wondering if it was her parents

152

calling from France. It was Hannah, eager to talk about an idea she'd had.

"It's not even eight o'clock, Hannah," Amy said. "My eyes aren't open yet."

"It's a lovely morning," Hannah rushed on. "And as I'm not working today, why don't we take Pedro to Greenwich? I've rung Callum and he's keen."

Amy liked the idea. "You'll have to give me a couple of hours to get ready."

"You ring Pedro and let him know," said Hannah. "Callum'll pick him up at ten."

"OK."

"And I'll come round to your place in about an hour."

"An hour?" Amy protested. "I won't be ready in an hour."

"You'll *have* to be," Hannah demanded. "I need to talk to you before the boys arrive."

She put down the receiver before Amy had had a chance to reply.

Amy slumped into a chair at the kitchen table and looked up at Hannah with tears in her eyes.

"I didn't mean to hurt you," said Hannah. She knelt beside the chair and put her arm around her best friend. "It's just that Callum was getting worried. I'm sure he's wrong, but . . . well, he asked me to talk to you about it."

The tears began to run down Amy's cheeks. "He's not wrong, Hannah," she said, softly.

Hannah was shocked. "You don't mean you've got a thing about Pedro?"

"I don't know," she sighed. She gripped Hannah's hand. "I love Michael, Hannah. Really, I do. But he's not here and. . ."

"And Pedro?" Hannah asked quickly. "What does he feel about this?"

"Nothing," said Amy. "I don't think Pedro has any idea how I feel about him. How can he? I'm not even sure how I feel about him *myself*. Anyway, he told me last week that he's in love with some Spanish girl. So nothing can possibly happen between us. Thank goodness." The tears flowed faster. "Oh Hannah," she sobbed. "If only Michael was here. If only he hadn't gone away."

"He'll be back soon." Hannah tried to comfort her. "And everything will be just as it *was*. You'll see."

"No, it won't," cried Amy. "It can't be."

"Don't be silly," said Hannah. "Of course it can."

"But you don't understand." Amy wiped her tears on a crumpled tissue.

Hannah saw just how serious Amy looked. This was something terrible, she was sure. "What is it?" she asked, concerned. "Tell me, Amy. What don't I understand?"

"I've done something really silly," Amy explained. "And I'm in a bit of a mess about it."

"Tell me."

"About a week ago, I wrote a letter to Michael," she sobbed, "and. . . Oh God, I wish I hadn't."

"What sort of letter?" enquired Hannah. "What do you mean?"

The doorbell rang.

"Oh, no!" gasped Amy.

"That's them," said Hannah. "Look, I'll open the door while you go up to the bathroom and sort yourself out. You don't want them to see you in that state. We'll talk later, eh?"

Amy hurriedly left the room while Hannah went to open the front door.

As the bus pulled into Seville, Michael was horrified. The unattractive blocks of flats which littered the skyline weren't quite what he'd expected to see. However, the walk to Conchita and Juan's grandparents' house soon changed his opinion of the city. Every corner they turned brought more and more delights: elegant old houses with patios and courtyards filled with all kinds of brightly-coloured, exotic plants. The streets were lined with small orange trees, and the people going about their daily business beneath the bright blue, cloudless sky, seemed happy and content.

They walked to the Plaza España and across the park, passing the many fountains and palms, which were filled with cooing white doves . . . and on to the large white house where the Spanish flag flew above its portal.

"This is it," said Conchita. She threw her bag over one shoulder and grabbed Michael's hand, dragging him excitedly along the path towards the smiling, grey-haired woman, standing on the steps which led to the front door, arms opened wide, waiting to greet her grandchildren. Juan overtook them, leaping up the steps and tightly hugging his grandma.

As Michael was introduced, the old woman kissed him on both cheeks, spoke rapidly in undecipherable Spanish and beckoned him into her palatial home, where he was given a plate of soup and crusty bread accompanied by a small glass of sherry. Having spoken in his now much-improved Spanish to Juan and Conchita's parents and grandparents, he was shown to a dark and cool, high-ceilinged bedroom where he was left to make himself comfortable before taking a quick tour around the city.

They arrived at Greenwich station around eleven o'clock and walked to the market, where they looked at the clothes, the bric-à-brac and the tacky tourist souvenirs. The sky was a cloudless, bright blue, as it had been for most of the summer, and all four wore just T-shirts and shorts.

Hannah had felt disturbed throughout the journey, wondering what exactly Amy had put in the letter to Michael. She'd glanced across the train carriage at her from time to time, giving her a reassuring smile and hoping that there would be some time during the day when they could talk. Amy too was desperate, but she knew that her full confession to Hannah would have to wait until after the trip. Maybe they'd be able to talk later that evening, if, somehow, they could persuade the boys to go elsewhere and leave them alone for a few hours.

"Here, this'll look really good on you," laughed Callum as he picked up a bright pink, wide-brimmed hat from one of the market stalls. He turned and placed it on Amy's head, much to the annoyance of the vendor who realized they had no intention of buying anything.

"Better on me," said Pedro as he grabbed the hat and placed it on his own head. "A pink sombrero."

As they all hooted with laughter, the vendor stepped forward and gently removed the hat from Pedro's head, placing it back on the stall.

They strolled on towards the *Cutty Sark* where Callum, having read notes on the great sailing vessel from a small tourists' handbook, passed the information on to Pedro.

"I hope you're listening to this too, girls," Callum said with a grin. "We don't want Pedro thinking you're two little English ignoramuses, do we?"

Hannah laughed and took Callum's arm, gently propelling him towards the river's barrier, where the four of them leaned over the rail and watched the swans gliding up the Thames towards Tower Bridge.

"Aren't they beautiful?" said Amy.

"Yes. And they mate for life, you know," Callum replied as he lovingly gripped Hannah's hand. "Unlike many humans, when swans get together, it really is 'till death us do part'."

Amy sighed. "What a lovely thought. I bet one of them won't be flying off to Spain and leaving the other one behind, though," she added.

The others fell silent.

They walked into Greenwich Park and stopped outside the Observatory, studying the Greenwich Mean Time line.

Amy grinned at Pedro. "I hope you don't want an explanation of how the world's time is all measured from here," she said. "Because I wouldn't know where to start."

"Don't worry," Pedro grinned back. "I know all about it." He laughed. "I wonder how much you can tell me about Madrid's Puerta Del Sol?"

They all looked at each other, blankly.

"Not a lot," said Callum.

Pedro beamed. "As I thought," he said. "English ignoramus."

Hannah screeched with laughter and pointed at Callum. "There! You ignoramus. It's not just me and Amy."

"Right!" said Callum. "Calling me names, eh?" He smirked mischievously. "See these?" He held up his fingers in front of her face.

"Yes?" she said, smiling at him. "They're really bony, aren't they?"

"They make the most wonderful tickling machine, though," he added.

"Don't you dare!" she shrieked.

He leaped at her and she sped away from him, screaming and laughing loudly. He chased after her, racing along the path and across the field, where they caused a group of Japanese tourists to turn and laugh at the antics of these young English lovers.

Catching up with her, he pulled her down on to the grass and lay on top of her, gripping her tightly with one hand as he lifted the other hand, ready to tickle her.

"Please, don't, Callum!" she yelped. "I can't stand being tickled. It hurts."

He stopped, lowered his hand and looked into her eyes. "Would I do anything to hurt you?" he asked, softly.

She whispered back, "I hope not."

He pressed his lips to hers and kissed her, passionately.

Pedro and Amy, who'd been following them across the

field, suddenly stopped in their tracks and sat where they were.

"I think they'd be better off without us, don't you?" said Pedro as he and Amy gazed down towards the Maritime Museum and at the magnificent views of London, sprawled out beyond it.

A small boy whooped joyfully as he raced by them, holding on tightly to the strings of a small kite.

Amy was lost in thought.

"Are you all right?" Pedro asked her.

"I'm fine," she lied.

Having lazed in the park all day, the four left by the top gate leading to Blackheath where the fairground, with its flashing lights and loud music, looked inviting.

Feeling hungry, they bought burgers and chips and wandered around the rides, trying to decide which were the most appealing.

"Oh, look!" exclaimed Hannah, as she saw the row of teddy bears sitting on a high shelf behind one of the stalls. "I want one!" she cried childlike . . . and with a twinkle in her eye, she added, "Will you win me one, Callum?"

They all laughed.

Callum tutted and smiled. "How do you expect me to win one of those?" he asked. He eyed the pile of tin cans which had to be knocked down by throwing three tiny, soft beanbags. "Nobody ever wins on those things."

"Half those cans will be stuck down," Pedro agreed.

The stallholder approached; "No, they're not," he said, aggressively. "People only say they're *stuck* down when they haven't got the strength to *knock* 'em down."

"I'll have a go," Callum said immediately.

He paid his money, picked up the three beanbags and hurled each one at the centre pile of tin cans. The first two throws were very successful, to squeals of delight from Amy and Hannah. The third beanbag hit the cans with great force, but they refused to budge.

"Told you," Callum whispered. "It's impossible."

The stallholder approached them with three more beanbags. "Why don't you have a go?" he asked Pedro. "You're probably stronger than yer mate!"

"I don't think so," Pedro grinned.

"Go on, Pedro," said Callum. "It's probably tactics rather than strength."

Pedro laughed loudly. "Oh, sure!" He paid for the beanbags and hurled them at the reset pile of tin cans.

On the third throw, the last of the remaining cans tumbled over with a crash.

Callum was shocked. Pedro beamed and punched the air. And the two girls jumped up and down, screeching excitedly.

The stallholder picked up one of the teddy bears and handed it to Pedro. "Told yer!" he said, with a grin. "You're tougher than yer mate!"

Pedro immediately handed the teddy bear to Hannah.

"For you," he said.

"And now. . ." said Amy, dramatically, "the big wheel! Who thinks they're brave enough?"

"Why not?" replied Hannah. She put her arm through Amy's and both girls wandered across the fair towards the big wheel, leaving the boys to trail behind them.

"Are you OK?" Hannah asked, quietly.

"Not really," replied Amy. "But we can't talk about it now. Tonight, hopefully." She sighed deeply. "I can't believe I've been so stupid."

"Whatever it is," said Hannah, "I'm sure it can't be as bad as you think."

She stopped suddenly, when she felt Callum's hand ruffle her hair from behind.

"I like to rock the carriage," he lied. "So I hope you're not going to embarrass me by screaming."

She smiled at him with a twinkle in her eye. "Likewise!" she replied.

As Pedro and Amy climbed into a carriage on the big wheel, Amy was quiet.

Pedro gently took her hand. "Are you all right?" he asked.

She smiled at him and tightly gripped on to his fingers as their carriage rose in the air a few metres and then stopped. She waved down to Hannah and Callum who climbed into the carriage below them.

As the ride began, Pedro, never fond of heights, wrapped his arm around Amy. They gazed down at the other fairground rides and the caravans and the people, all beginning to shrink in size.

Hannah sat the teddy bear on the seat beside them as she cuddled up to Callum.

"I hate these things," she said, half-giggling, though fear was written in her eyes.

Callum laughed. "Me too."

"Then why did you come on it?" asked Hannah, surprised.

"I thought *you* wanted to," he said. "I would never have come on here otherwise."

She snuggled up closer and sighed contentedly. "You'll be telling me next that you'd walk through fire for me," she said.

His sigh echoed hers. "I probably would," he replied.

Hannah constantly watched the clock, wondering how she could persuade Callum and Pedro to leave . . . and allow her some time with Amy. It was eleven o'clock already. On returning to Amy's house, they'd all agreed to go in for a quick cup of coffee. But that was three hours ago. And now, engrossed in conversation, the boys appeared to have no intention of leaving.

"Shall I make some more coffee?" Amy asked, finally.

Hannah shook her head and yawned. "Not for me. I'll help you wash these mugs up. I've got to be home soon. I'm working tomorrow."

"I've got a better idea," suggested Pedro. "Callum can take you home, Hannah, and I'll stay and help Amy wash up."

Amy was quick to respond. "No. Don't worry about that, Pedro," she said. "Callum can take you home too. I don't need any help to wash up a few mugs."

Callum looked at Hannah. He didn't want to leave Pedro alone with Amy. But he didn't know how to get him to leave, without causing offence. Hannah too, felt helpless. She didn't know how to handle the situation.

"I insist," said Pedro. "I will enjoy it. I never have to wash up in Madrid." He gave a broad smile. "The maids do everything."

Hannah looked at Amy who shrugged, resignedly.

"I'll give you a call tomorrow, Amy," she said pointedly. "As soon as I've finished work."

And as she and Callum left, she turned back to see the haunted look in Amy's eyes.

Juan decided to stay and talk to his relatives as Conchita

showed Michael some of the more important sights of Seville. They gazed up at the Giralda, the incredible Moorish bell tower, before entering the cathedral to inspect the tomb of Christopher Columbus. They strolled along the palm-tree-lined river, where the many horse-drawn carriages carried excited tourists. Then they headed on towards Carmen's famous tobacco factory, returning via the gardens of the Alcazar Real which were filled with gigantic palms and fruit trees, orange, lemon and banana. Here they sat on a stone bench, listening to the fountains splashing into the pond beside them, where dozens of fish rose to the surface devouring pieces of bread being thrown to them by a small boy. The boy's father smiled as he played a flamenco song on his guitar, watching another of his children, a pretty girl no older than four, dancing and swirling around as she clacked with confidence on a pair of bright red castanets.

"This was Pedro's favourite place," sighed Conchita as she threw back her head and held her face to the evening sun.

"It's beautiful," said Michael. "And it's so exciting."

Conchita shrugged. "For me, it's sad. Full of memories."

Michael took her hand and squeezed it affectionately. "But it doesn't have to be like that, Conchita," he said. "If you and Pedro still love each other, then it's ridiculous to be separated. I know you don't want to upset your parents, but it's *your* life.

And if being apart from Pedro makes you miserable, then you must stand up to them."

Conchita looked at her watch. "We must go," she said. "It's nine o'clock and we're meeting the family for dinner."

In a quiet courtyard at the back of a small bar, the family sat around a long wooden table, chatting and sipping at *sangría* as they waited for the bartender to bring them some *tapas* and bread as a starter.

"I wonder how my little Pedro is?" said Conchita's grandmother. "I hope he's enjoying England."

"He's having a wonderful time, Grandma," Conchita replied confidently. "He's really enjoying it there."

Michael almost choked on his drink. He stared incredulously at Conchita, who returned his stare with a nervous flicker of a smile. Juan looked across at Michael, wide-eyed with disbelief.

"So, he's written to you?" asked Conchita's mother. "I'm so pleased. I still can't believe that you stopped seeing him."

"I thought you were made for each other," added her father. "The perfect couple."

Grandma looked concerned as she reached across the table and took Conchita's hand. "What *did* go wrong?" she asked. "I was very upset to hear that your relationship was over. He's such a nice boy, Conchita."

Conchita forced a smile as she quickly wiped away a tear with her free hand.

"If you can discover the truth, Mama," said Conchita's mother, "then you're a better woman than I."

"I really would like to change the subject," pleaded Conchita. "Pedro and I are finished as a couple. I hope we will continue to be friends, but we can never be really close again." She took out her handkerchief and dabbed her eyes. "Will you excuse me for a moment?" she said as she left the table and headed towards the bar.

Michael watched her go, shocked at the realization that Conchita's parents had nothing to do with the break-up.

Why had she lied? What *was* the truth?

Fifteen

The family strolled back through the winding Sevillano streets, and on reaching the house they said their goodnights. When Juan suggested that he and Michael sit in the garden for a while, sipping some cool lemonade, Michael readily agreed. It was far too humid to sleep, even though it was nearing midnight. Conchita joined them, sitting on the old garden swing, which had been placed there years before for the enjoyment of Juan and Conchita when they were still toddlers.

Juan and Michael flopped on to the small wrought-iron bench, facing the swing.

"So, tell me," said Juan, sounding annoyed with his sister, "what was that all about? *Has* Pedro been writing to you?"

Conchita looked down at her feet as she swung gently to and fro.

"Conchita?" he said. "I'm confused. Please, tell me."

"No," she replied in a whisper. "He hasn't written to me."

"I don't understand," said Michael. "Then why did you say he had?"

She looked up at them and began to raise her voice. "Because I'm sick of the questions. I'm sick of being reprimanded by everyone for ending the relationship with Pedro. I thought if I said that we were still friends, then the matter would be dropped . . . at least for this evening."

Juan sipped on his lemonade. "But now Mama and Papa will expect Pedro to visit us when he returns," he said. "And that will never happen, will it?"

Conchita rose from the swing and looked sadly at Juan. "No, he'll never visit." Tears filled her eyes. "I wish he *would*. I miss him. I wish he *had* written to me. But he hasn't. And he won't, unless. . ."

"Unless *you* write to *him*," interrupted Michael.

"I can't," she said. "It's too late, Michael. I can't do it. I've tried. But I can't."

Leaving the two boys staring after her, she walked slowly across the garden towards the house.

Juan and Michael sat in silence for a while, watching the stars and listening to the sound of the cicadas.

Juan finally broke the silence. "I hate to see her so unhappy. She was always such fun. When she and Pedro were together there was so much laughter. They were really good company."

Michael shrugged. "It's such a waste. When two people are in love like that, it seems nonsense to spend their time apart."

Juan smiled. "Like you and your English girlfriend."

"Amy? That's different," said Michael. "We're only apart for five weeks. We'll be back together soon."

"But you are unhappy without her."

"Yes, but I'm happy to have seen Spain."

"But you'd be happier to see Spain if she were with you."

"Of course," said Michael. "I'm worried that when I return to London, she'll have found someone else."

"Then perhaps you shouldn't stay away from her for quite so long," Juan lectured him.

Michael sighed. "I've been wondering about that. I think about her every day. I go to sleep with pictures of her in my head. And everything I see or do I want to share with her. I keep wanting to turn to her and say, 'Look at that, Amy,' or, 'Isn't that beautiful, Amy?' This visit is so exciting for me, Juan, and yet it's a part of my life that she can never share. Even though I write and tell her everything in detail, she can never *really* be part of it."

"If I had someone to love," said Juan, "I would never put myself through this torture. There's Pedro in England and Conchita here . . . a thousand miles apart. And the same for you and Amy."

"But hopefully, when I return, Amy will be waiting for me," replied Michael.

"*Hopefully*," said Juan, pointedly.

"But unless Conchita tells your parents to stop interfering in her life, then *she* and *Pedro* will never get back together."

"My parents?" asked Juan, surprised. "What have my parents got to do with it?"

"Conchita's told me," replied Michael. "And so has Santi. Your mother and father don't approve of Pedro as a partner for Conchita because he's abandoned his Catholic faith."

Juan was horrified. "They told you that?"

"Yes. I was very surprised when they spoke of Pedro so affectionately after all they'd done to ruin the relationship."

"But it isn't true," said Juan. "My parents and my grandparents love Pedro. Santi was definitely mistaken. It was Conchita's decision. It was she who was distressed because Pedro wouldn't return to the church. Conchita was thinking of marriage and she felt that her future had to be spent with someone who shared her faith. It's Conchita's decision alone. My parents had nothing to do with it."

Michael felt angry. "Then she doesn't love him. Not really," he said bluntly.

"Oh, I think you're wrong," said Juan. "She loves him very much."

"No," Michael said softly. "She doesn't. She wants to control him. True love is unconditional. Conchita doesn't love Pedro for what he *is*, but for what she would *like* him to be."

"Yes. I understand what you're saying." Juan nodded solemnly. "My faith is very important to me, but if I fell in love with someone who didn't share the same faith, then I hope I would respect that person's way of life."

"You're right," said Conchita. Stepping from the shadows, where she'd listened to the whole conversation, she approached them. She knelt in front of the bench and looked up at Michael.

"I'm sorry, Conchita," said Michael. "It's got nothing to do with me. I have no right. . ."

She gently placed a hand on his knee. "You have every right, Michael. You're my friend, I hope."

"Conchita," he softly pleaded. "Write to him. Tell him how you feel. Don't throw your love away."

Juan agreed. "Remember all those wonderful times you and Pedro had together. I've never seen two happier people, Conchita. You may still have your differences, but that doesn't stop you loving each other for what you are. At least *try* to make it work."

Conchita smiled. "I've been thinking about it very deeply," she said. "I began to write to him when we returned from Segovia, but I tore the letter up. I couldn't express myself properly on paper. I'm not good at writing love letters."

"Well then, *call* him," said Michael. "Talk to him." He looked at his watch. "It's twelve-forty-five," he added. "So it's eleven-forty-five in London. He may still be up, talking to my parents. Call him *now*."

Conchita grinned broadly. She suddenly felt so happy, so confident about the future. "Why not?" she said. She grabbed Michael's hand and pulled him to his feet. "Tell me the number."

The three of them hurried up to the house. "I'll dial it for you," said Michael.

Pedro clumsily wiped each of the mugs which Amy handed to him.

"You're not very good at this, are you?" Amy laughed.

"Not very," grinned Pedro. "I haven't had much practice."

"You'd better get used to it," she said. "You may not always have maids."

"I don't want them," replied Pedro. "When I marry, I want a small house with a beautiful wife who will do everything for me. I wouldn't want to have maids getting in the way all the time."

Amy dropped the mug she was holding into the soapy water. "Oh, excuse me?" she said, harshly. "You want a wife to do everything for you? How about you and your wife working together? Or *you* doing everything for *her*?"

Pedro laughed. "But I will have to work. She will stay at home and have babies and look after the house."

Amy couldn't believe what she was hearing. "And suppose your wife wants a career?"

Pedro eyes twinkled. He was enjoying the joke. "But she can't," he said. "I can't have the babies, can I? That will be her job. I will have to go to work."

She said it without thinking, "And how did Conchita cope with that idea? Is that why she left you?"

He looked at her, sadly.

"I'm sorry," she said.

He tried to smile, quickly grabbing another mug from the draining-board. "I was only making fun," he informed her. "I was joking."

"Oh," she said. She felt deeply embarrassed. "I'm sorry," she repeated as she continued to wash up.

"Sorry for what? You don't have to be sorry."

She turned from the sink to face him. "Pedro. . . . ?"

"Yes?"

"Tell me why it ended," she said. "Why did you and Conchita separate? If you still love each other as you say you do, then I don't understand."

"Why do you want to know?" he asked her, softly.

"Because I'm selfish," she replied. "Because, if I'm truthful, I'm only thinking about myself."

"I don't know what you mean," he said. "Thinking about yourself? What do you mean by that?"

174

"Because if two people love each other and yet their relationship comes to an end. . ."

"Yes?"

"Then that could happen to Michael and me, couldn't it?" she said, fearfully.

Pedro smiled. "No," he said. "It's not the same situation at all. Conchita and I have a deep difference of opinion that keeps us apart."

"Such as?" she enquired.

"I'd better go," he said. "It's getting late. Michael's parents will be worried about me."

Amy looked up at the clock on the kitchen wall. "It's a quarter to twelve," she said. "Perhaps you'd better call them and tell them where you are."

"Perhaps I should," he agreed.

"It's engaged," said Michael, sounding surprised. He wondered who his parents could be talking to at such a late hour.

Conchita was distressed. Having finally plucked up the courage to speak to Pedro, she now had to put everything on hold. The adrenalin was surging through her body. Her heart was pounding.

"I'll try again," said Michael as he redialled the number. He waited. "Aah, it's ringing," he said.

Conchita's mouth was dry. How would she start the conversation? What was she going to say?

She and Juan listened as Michael spoke to his mother, quickly relating tales of Madrid, Segovia, Seville and his new-found friends.

"Can I speak to Pedro?" he asked eventually.

There was a pause.

"Oh!" he said. "Really?"

Having wished his mother goodnight, he put down the receiver with a trembling hand.

"What the matter?" asked Conchita, sounding very concerned.

"Pedro's not there," he informed her. "He hasn't got back yet."

Michael knew that Amy's parents would be in France by now. Pedro and Amy were together . . . alone . . . at her house. And it was almost midnight.

Sixteen

Having stacked the mugs and wiped the kitchen surfaces, Pedro sat over yet another cup of coffee and talked as he hadn't talked for months. Amy was a good listener and it felt good to unburden himself in this way.

"Why don't you write to her?" Amy asked. "Tell her everything you've told me."

He shrugged. "She'd probably just throw the letter away."

"But she may *not*, Pedro." Amy was doing her best to sound positive. "Surely it's worth a try? If you both love each other, it seems such a waste to let it all go."

"I wouldn't know where to start." He smiled. "I've never been good at writing love letters."

"I'll help you," she said. She leaped up from the table. "Why don't I get some paper? We could do it together; put down all your thoughts in writing."

She suddenly thought about the last letter she'd sent to

Michael and she felt the palms of her hands begin to sweat. Here she was, giving advice to a friend; helping him to write a love letter, when she was terrified that the last one *she'd* written had been a total disaster. She wished that she could explain everything to Pedro: how sick she was feeling inside and how worried she was that her final letter to Michael might have ended their relationship.

With a trembling hand, she placed the paper and a pen in front of him. "Let's start," she said. "*Dear Conchita. . .*"

Conchita quietly left the house, looking back at the lamp glowing softly through her bedroom window. The other rooms were in darkness, its inhabitants sleeping soundly. She strolled very slowly into the town, passing many who, like herself, couldn't sleep on this humid Andalucian night.

She gazed up at the moon, almost full, and at the thousands of stars which surrounded it, and she thought of the nights that she and Pedro had strolled hand in hand beneath this very sky and had talked about their future together. It had taken hours to compose the letter which she was gripping tightly in her hand and yet she still wasn't sure if she'd have the courage to post it. She wanted Pedro back. Badly. There'd been no happiness in her life since he'd left. And Michael was right. True love shouldn't carry conditions.

She'd loved Pedro for what he was and she had no right to impose her ideals on him.

When she'd asked Michael for the address, both he and Juan had seemed delighted. Then, shut away in her room, she'd written what she really felt for Pedro. But could she actually send the letter? She reached the mail box, hovered for a while . . . and then walked on. She stopped and turned back. Then, with great trepidation, she sealed the envelope with a kiss . . . and sent it on its way to London.

Hannah put out her hand and gripped Amy's. "Tell me," she said. "I can't help you if I don't know what's going on, can I?"

As the tears rolled, Amy explained how she'd been confused about her feelings for Pedro and about the letter she'd sent to Michael.

Hannah gasped. "Oh Amy. You didn't!"

"Nothing happened between me and Pedro," she said. "Really. He didn't even know how I felt. Thank goodness he didn't because I don't feel that way any more. He's just a good friend, Hannah, and he's totally in love with his Spanish girlfriend."

"But why did you send the letter?" asked Hannah. "I can't believe you did that."

"Me neither," sobbed Amy. "It was the most stupid thing I've ever done. I was just feeling so lost without Michael and

179

so muddled up about everything." She took out a tissue and dabbed her eyes. "Oh Hannah. What am I going to do?"

"You should've trusted me," Hannah scolded her. "I'm your best friend, Amy. You should've told me what you were going through and we could've talked. Then none of this would've happened."

"You were too busy," Amy replied. "What with work and Callum and. . ."

Hannah was upset. "But we're friends, Amy. We know everything about each other. I would've found time for you, no matter what else was going on in my life."

"I know, I know," said Amy.

Hannah gripped Amy's hand more tightly. "We tell each other everything. We always have." She immediately felt guilty. She hadn't told Amy of the relief she'd felt when Pedro had arrived on the scene. It had meant that, now they were a foursome again, Hannah would have Callum's full attention. She wouldn't have to share it with Amy.

"Perhaps we haven't been as open with each other as we should've been," added Hannah, sadly. "And we *must* be, Amy. In future. Neither Callum nor Michael must come between us, no matter how much we love them. Our friendship is too important."

"Yes," agreed Amy. "It is."

Both girls stood and hugged each other.

"Now," Hannah said softly, "what are we going to do about this letter you've sent to Michael?"

Pedro rang his mother as soon as she'd arrived home from work.

"And how's the English?" she asked.

"Good," he said. "It's getting better all the time. In fact, it's so good that I don't think I need to spend the full five weeks here."

She laughed. "You're feeling homesick?"

"A bit."

"And you're missing your mother."

"That too," he laughed back.

"Or could it be that you're missing someone else?" she asked.

"You haven't seen her, have you?"

"No. Not for a few days." She wondered if she should tell Pedro that Conchita was in Seville with her brother . . . and Michael, but fearing that it might hurt him if she delivered such a message over the phone, she decided to change the subject. "So tell me all about London. Is it raining there as usual?"

"It's been very warm and sunny, actually," he replied. "Though not as hot as Madrid, I'm sure. Listen," he added, "will you do me a big favour, without asking any questions?"

"Now, that depends," she replied.

"Is there a letter there for Michael, postmarked from London?"

"Yes. What about it?" she was curious.

"Will you destroy it, please?"

"Destroy it? I can't do that," she said.

"Please, Mama," he said. "You'll be doing a very kind service to two people. You may even prevent a relationship from ending in tears."

"It's that serious?"

"It's that serious."

"Don't tell your father what I've done," she said.

He laughed. "I promise."

"So, are you staying the full course?" she asked. "We can hardly ask Michael to vacate your room. Shall we make up a spare bed?"

"Give me a few days to think about it," he replied.

Michael returned from Seville, looking forward to opening the several letters that would surely be waiting for him. He was disturbed when Pedro's mother, somewhat guiltily, informed him that there hadn't been any post from London.

Throughout the morning he couldn't stop fretting, wondering if Amy had given up on him. He couldn't help worrying that she might have found someone else. And it crossed his mind that that someone else might be Pedro.

Conchita saw how gloomy he looked as soon as he walked into the Torito later that evening.

"You were very keen to advise *me*, Michael," she said with a comforting smile. "But are you as good at receiving advice?"

"Tell me," he said.

"Call her. There's a telephone just outside the bar. Call her and tell her you love her. Ask her if there's anything wrong."

"No, there's nothing wrong," she said. Her heart was pounding. "Oh, it's so wonderful to hear your voice, Michael."

"But you haven't written," he said, plaintively.

She beamed. So the letter *had* been destroyed as Pedro had promised. "I didn't see the point," she said. "You were in Seville. I didn't have an address there."

"Do you miss me?" he asked.

"I miss you like crazy, Michael."

"I miss you too," he said. "It's beautiful here, but it's pointless when I can't share it with you."

"Only another couple of weeks," she mused, "and we'll be together again."

"Maybe sooner," he replied.

She was startled. "Sooner?"

183

"What would you say if I told you I was thinking of coming back earlier?"

"Are you kidding?"

"I'm deadly serious."

"When?" she asked, excitedly.

"As soon as I can get a flight."

She sighed. "Oh Michael!"

"Will you meet me at the airport?"

"Try keeping me away."

The doorbell rang just as she put down the phone. She shrieked with joy and raced along the hall. She was expecting Hannah to call round and she couldn't wait to tell her the news. She was surprised to see Pedro, standing on the step, beaming at her and holding up a letter.

"I've got wonderful news," he said.

She grinned at him. "You and me both. Come in. I'll put the kettle on."

"Well?" asked Conchita. "Was she there?"

"Yes," said Michael. "And everything's fine." He paused, took Conchita's hand and stared into the dark green eyes. "I think I'm going home," he said. "I can't bear to be without her any longer."

She smiled at him. "A good idea."

"Perhaps Pedro will do the same," he said, only half-convinced.

"He will," she replied, confidently.

He gazed at her. "Is there something you're not telling me?"

She laughed. "I wrote to him from Seville as you suggested," she said. "I told him that I wanted to start again. With no conditions."

Michael flung his arms round her and whooped loudly. "Well done!"

"And even better than that," she added. "Look." From her pocket she took out a letter. "He must have written to me at the same time." Her green eyes suddenly misted over. "He misses me, Michael. He wants to come home as soon as possible, to try and patch things up between us."

"He won't have to try very hard, will he?" grinned Michael.

"There's no patching up to be done," she said. "He's done nothing wrong. I want Pedro for Pedro's sake. I love him just the way he is."

Conchita stood silently at the arrival gate, waiting for the London to Madrid flight. Lost in her thoughts, past, present and future, she was almost oblivious to the conversation between Michael and Pedro's parents.

"Thank you for everything, Antonio," said Michael. "You and Suzana have made me so welcome."

"Any time, Michael," Antonio replied.

"And if you want to return and bring Amy with you," added Suzana, "just give us a call. *Our* house is *your* house."

Conchita gave a gasp and a tiny squeal as she saw Pedro pass through passport control.

"He's here," she yelled.

"I'll go," said Michael. "I have to board in ten minutes. He shook Antonio's hand and kissed Suzana on both cheeks. "Thanks again."

He gently placed an arm round Conchita's neck, kissed her quickly on the cheek and without waiting for a response, he hurried away towards the departure gate.

"I *told* you it was the first thing we'd do when I got home from Spain," said Michael.

"Our pact," added Callum.

The fire crackled and burned even brighter than the first fire they'd built here.

"Let's just hope that Callum's car starts this time," laughed Amy as she huddled closer to Michael, watching the sparks fly.

"It wouldn't matter to me if it *didn't* start," said Michael. "Who wants to go home?"

"I wouldn't mind staying here for ever and ever," agreed Callum. "Just like this. Me and Hannah. And you two. Lost in our own little Heaven." He sighed deeply. "I bet you're all glad that I showed you this place, aren't you?"

"We certainly are, Callum," Michael grinned. "Perhaps we should come back here at this time every year. On our anniversaries." He laughed. "An annual trip to Bluebell Wood."

Hannah looked around her and smiled. "Not a lot of bluebells, are there?"

"Does it bother you?" asked Callum.

"Not in the least," replied Hannah

"Nor me," added Amy.

Michael lay down beside the glowing embers of the fire, pulled Amy towards him and wrapped his arms round her.

"Me neither," he said.